AHMEK

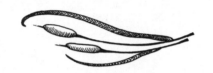

PATRICK WATSON

AHMEK

McArthur & Company
Toronto

This paperback edition published in 2004 by
McArthur & Company
322 King St. West, Ste 402
Toronto, ON
M5V 1J2
www.mcarthur-co.com

National Library of Canada Cataloguing in Publication

Watson, Patrick, 1929-
Ahmek / Patrick Watson ; Tracy Thomson, illustrator.

Originally published: North York, Ont. : Stoddart Kids, c1999.

ISBN 1-55278-417-7

1. Thomson, Tom, 1877-1917—Juvenile fiction. 2.
Beavers—Juvenile fiction. I. Thomson, Tracey, 1967- II. Title.

PS8595.A85A74 2004   jC813'.54   C2004-900859-5

The publisher would like to acknowledge the financial support of
the Government of Canada through the Book Publishing Industry
Development Program, The Canada Council for the Arts, and the
Ontario Arts Council for our publishing activities. We also
acknowledge the Government of Ontario through the Ontario
Media Development Corporation Ontario Book Initiative.

Cover illustration: Tracy Thomson
Printed and bound in Canada by Friesens

CONTENTS

FOREWORD

If you ever find yourself paddling a canoe across a certain lake in Algonquin Park at five o'clock of an August morning, as I did once when I was a boy, keeping your eye on the North Star straight ahead to guide you . . . and if the full moon is close to setting in the west, and the fog bank rolling out of the little bay in the northeast corner sits like a wall in the middle of that lake . . . you may see the same ghost that I saw, out of the corner of my eye, too scared to turn and look right at it.

Paddling right beside me, in a pale grey canoe, his paddle making not a sound, but matching me stroke for stroke. Sending the hair up on the back of my neck as I guessed who it must be.

Until I realized that it was my moonshadow on the solid wall of fog beside me.

And one day, much later, remembering that ghost, and the wall of fog rolling out of that little bay at the northeast corner, I began to peer behind that wall of fog. And I found a story there. And if you peer behind that wall with me, you can come into the story too.

Here it is.

ONE   *Danger!*

Ahmek slipped silently out of the lower entrance to
the lodge, into the cool, dark water of Wiyaunuk.
The bottom of the pond was dappled with sunlight.
Underwater Ahmek's fur carried an iridescent shimmer
of fine air bubbles. He had been sleeping on his bed of
shredded bark in the dry upper chamber of the lodge,
and his fur was still dry enough that bubbles of air
stuck to its tiny barbs until Ahmek picked up speed.
Then the bubbles washed off or dissolved in the depths
of Wiyaunuk.

Ahmek had heard some unfamiliar murmur and
faint liquid plashing sounds, dimly coming through the
mud and stick walls of the lodge. He had exchanged
soft questioning whimpers with N'Osse, his father.
N'Osse had wakened N'Okomis, Ahmek's grandmother,
who sleepily listened to what Ahmek described. She

thought about it silently for a while.

Ahmek and his father waited patiently for her thoughts to form, because she was the Grandmother.

Finally she said, "Ahmek, go and see what it is about. Go slowly and go silently." Then N'Okomis rolled over back to sleep, and Ahmek slipped into the plunge hole and down the packed earth tunnel towards the bottom of the pond.

Even before he came close enough to the surface to see it clearly, a dark shape above, an alien shape, sent instinctive signals of watchfulness through Ahmek's nerves. There was a dim memory connected to this shape. A puzzling memory: something about his mother, about the Ningoshkauwin (that time when she went out to repair the dam and did not come back again). Something about that shape.

Ahmek let the air in his lungs expand and ascended warily, gazing up at the shadow.

The shape came into focus, a round grey . . . *belly* sort of shape, long like a log, but coming to a rounded point at each end.

Under the water, the shape was clear. But Ahmek could tell that there was a great deal more of it above the water. It was not an ordinary log. Faint ripples around its edge and an indistinct shape above scattered off into flakes, some of them iridescent, too, as the sunlight broke through the ripples. In the water, scarcely moving, near one end of the long grey log shape, there was a pale, flat, rounded thing. This thing resembled Ahmek's tail. Flat. It stirred lightly, swirling the water just the way his tail often did. The log moved slowly away from him, turning as it did.

Ahmek's curiosity was drawing him irresistibly to the surface. Closer and closer he came to the strange log. But before he actually broke water, his wariness began to make him tremble. He paused. He *had* to see this thing.

After a moment Ahmek dived silently to the bottom of Wiyaunuk, five yards down. He skimmed close over the sodden black leaves and twigs left over from last year's foraging for food, above the weeds and the stones. He took himself well away from the shape.

Down here he could no longer see it, but he knew the bottom of the pond so well that he knew exactly where the shape was and exactly how much distance he must put between it and himself.

He came up, up, slowly, slowly. He eased his nose and his dark, intense eyes above the surface without a ripple. He looked at the alien thing, now about forty yards away.

It was longer than their lodge, but thinner. It was the colour of a beech tree: a soft, smooth grey. It was *like* a log. It was not alive. But there was something alive on it. An animal.

The animal was crouched forward on the grey log. No, *in* it, really, Ahmek saw, puzzled. A big animal. Not as big as Mukwoh the Bear. But big. Dangerous too, he felt.

He could not see any eyes. The animal's back was towards him. The animal was a strange colour as well; most of it was the colour of the sky, except the head, which was the colour of sand. There was fur on the top of its head, dark brown fur, something like his own.

He watched silently. The animal was holding a long,

thin, pale branch of yellow wood in the water. Someone must have peeled it to eat the bark. It glistened wetly.

The animal lifted the branch clear of the water and Ahmek could see the flat tail shape now, on the end of the branch. The same one he had seen from below. The flat wooden tail went back into the water and the animal moved it; the grey log turned slowly towards Ahmek.

And then a fearful thing happened. A light wisp of morning breeze came down from the hill above the east end of the pond, a faint breeze, only enough to cause the water to shimmer for an instant, to reflect some of the iridescence into Ahmek's eyes from the dancing light of the low sun. It was still early morning, a morning breeze.

But that was not the fearful part. The breeze reached Ahmek's nose. It carried a terrible scent, the animal's scent. Suddenly Ahmek's memory was vivid and full of alarm, his body tense. He clearly remembered his mother telling him about that smell. They had been on Okwanim, the dam, where its stout wall of sticks and packed mud had mysteriously broken in the night, sticks and mud ripped away, and the water of Wiyaunuk pouring through furiously.

"*Remember that scent, Ahmek!*" his mother had said. She said it so gravely that he knew this was one of the Greater Lessons, a lesson greater than stripping the bark from twigs, a lesson greater than squeezing water from your fur, a lesson as great as holding your breath, as great as . . . diving.

"Remember that scent, Ahmek. For that is the scent of a Human. And the Human is the Great Enemy, the greatest of all the enemies. Greater than Kahminik the Wolf, who cannot dive, greater than Bezhen the Lynx or Waubezhaesh the Marten. Watch, study, be ready to run, to swim.

"Even, Ahmek . . .," she said slowly, "even be ready to leave the pond." And that was a terrible thing to even think about, let alone to say out loud. *To leave the pond!*

That next morning, he remembered, Okwanim had been broken again, the water level going down fast. His mother had gone out to begin the repairs.

Ahmek and his father and grandmother had gone up the north slope to cut saplings for her. And then, when they came to the dam, Oh, Oh, Oh!

They had only been away a short time, not very long at all. Ahmek and his father and grandmother came dragging the saplings with them to join his mother at the work. The scent of Human was everywhere. Ahmek's mother was gone. That was the awful Ningoshkauwin of their family history, the disappearance. She was never seen again.

Ahmek could scarcely remember her face. She had silver tips on the fine hairs around her ears, hairs that shone in the moonlight especially, and silver whiskers. That was special. Her own mother called her Silvertips.

But that was long, long ago, and now there were immediate matters to deal with.

The grey log with the animal . . . *in* it . . . was still turning, turning towards him. And now he could see the animal's eyes come up, seeking, seeking, darting menace towards him. Involuntarily his back arched up, and his broad tail slapped the water with a fine, sharp, warning slap. He plunged towards the bottom of Wiyaunuk faster than a sinking stone.

The man chuckled softly. "This is going to take some patience," he said quietly to himself.

The man shifted in the canoe and sent it gently towards the shore with two graceful strokes of the paddle. He leaned forwards to shift a box made of oiled wood and wrapped in rags that were stained with blotches of dull colour. The box smelled of something like pine gum. There was a small sack behind this box. The man took a package from the sack, slipped down to sit on the bottom of the canoe, leaned backwards comfortably against the thwart with the paddle as a backrest, put his feet up, opened the package, and began to eat. Ahmek saw nothing of this. But someone else was watching. Ningik the Otter had surfaced on the other side of the pond within minutes of Ahmek's leaving.

"What is this?" Ningik said to himself. "This looks like fun. I better go and tell Ahmek."

TWO   *Now What?*

Within a second after the slap of his tail had shat-
tered the silence of Wiyaunuk, Ahmek was at the
bottom. His powerful webbed hind feet drove him
straight towards the lower entrance to the lodge. The
lodge was invisible, fifty yards away, but its position
was as certain in his mind as if it were there before him
in the clear sunlight and he in sunlight too, safely, sun-
ning, basking, looking over the whole acreage of his
home water instead of sculling in terror for the safety
of the lodge.

Once there, he whimpered out the story to his
father and grandmother, that there was this terrible
thing, this Human, that had come upon Wiyaunuk
their Water. His grandmother, N'Okomis, stopped
yawning when she heard Ahmek's description of the
animal. Her eyes narrowed. She said, "*Aabideg.* It must

be so. It is a Human. I have never seen one myself, but once, long ago, your grandfather, N'Mishomiss, was chased by one, on the ground. He told me about it, so I know. It is a terrible thing that you have seen."

She said, "It did not go near Okwanim? Okwanim is not broken? Wiyaunuk is not pouring through a hole in Okwanim?"

Ahmek shook his head. He didn't *think* so. But he felt uneasy because, well, he had not really gone to the dam. You always went to the dam first, if there were signs. But he had let himself be distracted by the Human in the log. Now surely he would have heard something if the dam were broken and water rushing through. He would have seen if the level of Wiyaunuk was dropping, he thought. Surely.

The three beavers crouched silently in the shadowy lodge and thought this all over. A dull creamy light filtered weakly through the woven sticks at the top. A fairly large mound of sticks, making up the roof of the lodge, was above water. Inside this part was the sleeping chamber. A few inches below it and to one side was the drying and grooming chamber, where the family store of fresh food was stacked, and also where they met to groom each other's coats and talk things over. The sun had warmed and dried the mud that bound this roof together. It was like clay. Enough light came through this clay to let the beavers see each other. There was an air hole, too — a vent. For a few minutes each day, if the sun was shining, a brilliant shaft would fire the floor of the sleeping chamber with dancing white light, move slowly across the bedding of shavings and grasses and shredded bark, and then eclipse again.

Presently N'Osse, Ahmek's father, said, "What is your wisdom on this, N'Okomis, my mother? Do we need to make a magic and hear from the great spirit of the Beaver people? Or call on Nanabush the Protector? Or can we make our own safety here?"

N'Okomis was silent for a bit. Then she settled down and yawned and said, "We need to see this more clearly. We will wait awhile and then go out together and view the animal from different parts of Wiyaunuk.

"If it is still there," she added, after a moment, talking to herself more than to them. "Perhaps it will go away."

N'Okomis yawned again sleepily and rubbed her old eyes. "First we will have a little more sleep," she said. "I don't very much like going out in the daytime anyway."

She waddled her broad, fifty-pound bulk thoughtfully towards her bed. She paused by the food store and sniffed at the fresh poplar twigs. Picking out a very tender one, N'Okomis sniffed it again dreamily, took it in her mouth, closed her eyes and sighed a few times, continued to her bed, and settled her fur around her. She chewed contentedly at the twig and moved her tail from side to side until it was comfortable, until the arthritis in her back stopped irritating her. She swallowed her snack. Then she went off to sleep, just like that.

Ahmek and his father looked at each other and shrugged. "N'Okomis usually says the wise thing," Ahmek mewed. N'Osse nodded yes, and then he dozed off too, just like that.

When N'Okomis woke up she announced that she had had a dream and that she now wanted to go and take a look at the intruder all on her own, without them. Before they had time to comment she slipped into the plunge hole and was gone. N'Osse went back to sleep.

A few minutes later, outside the lodge, underwater, at the lower entrance to the plunge hole, Ningik the Otter stuck his head into the tunnel and listened. He could faintly hear sleep-breathing. He started quietly up the tunnel, staying in the water and trying not to make a sound. But when he came to the top, Ahmek was at the ledge just above the water, waiting for him, his eyes full of curiosity.

"I heard your bubbles," Ahmek said. "I can't come out to play now. I am waiting here with N'Osse until we decide what to do about that Human out there. My grandmother has gone for a look. Did you see the Human?"

Ningik nodded, of course he had seen it. He didn't miss anything, this Ningik.

"Scary, isn't it?" Ahmek said. But Ningik just shrugged. He travelled a lot more than the beavers did. He was used to watching Humans paddle by in their open logs, out in Zaaghigan, the big lake nearby. Humans didn't bother him, but he didn't have to worry about the water level in a pond or broken sticks in a dam. He liked the way Humans moved so rapidly, fast and quiet, along the surface. However, he felt a bit sorry for them that they couldn't move under the water with the same fluid speed that he could.

"I think I will go and look at this Human some more," Ningik said. "He doesn't look very scary to me."

And he sank down into the black water of the entrance tunnel and disappeared. Ahmek's sharp ears could hear the faint swirl as Ningik's tail and webbed feet propelled the otter smoothly out into Wiyaunuk. The water at the top of the tunnel swelled and receded with his going.

"Humm," Ahmek said silently to himself. "I wish I could go with him. When is N'Okomis coming back? It's been a long time."

Outside, Ningik came to the surface and looked across to where the Human had been lying in the grey log, only a few minutes ago. Now the grey log was pulled up on shore. The Human was sitting on a stone, with some sticks in front of it like three small trees leaning together in a swamp. A flat piece of wood was fastened upright on the sticks. The Human was staring hard at the flat piece of wood. Then it looked out across Wiyaunuk towards where Ningik had surfaced. Then it stared at the board again. Then it did a very strange thing. It took a small thin stick and pushed it at the flat piece of wood.

Now Ningik was pretty far away, floating beside a small deadhead that concealed him very well because his little nose and forehead looked like a lump on the old log. His eyesight was not as good out of the water as it was below, but even so, even at that distance, he could see bright red wetness on the end of the stick the Human was pushing at the flat piece of wood. The red wetness was the colour of the cardinal flowers on the bank behind him, which divided Wiyaunuk from Mushkeeg, the swamp, with its twisted black stems of small swamp spruce.

The Human looked across towards Mushkeeg and the deadhead and back at the board. It made another poke with the red wetness on the stick. Then it suddenly looked up, put its front paw over its eyes to shade them, and peered, sharp . . . right at Ningik's deadhead!

It was still for a moment, then called something out in an easy, friendly voice. "Hello, Ningik." This Human apparently knew the proper names for animals.

Ningik did not move. But he did not feel fear, either. He felt hunger, though.

He thought, I'll see if there are some crayfish on this bank. He dived and searched for a while and found three crayfish. Feeling quite safe, he came up on the deadhead and crawled clear of the water. Now the Human could certainly see him. Ningik crunched the crayfish with his sharp teeth and swallowed them. The Human saw all this, but now it was absorbed with its flat board and its little stick with a wet end, green now, Ningik thought, dark green. So Ningik washed his forepaws and wiped his whiskers. He arched his back and spread his hind legs for a moment, and then slipped back into the water and swam towards the Human for a better look.

The man did not look up. He stared at his board. After a while he said to himself, "Tom Thomson, that is really not too bad at all. Not too bad at all. Funny how a bit of smelly swamp by a beaver pond can suddenly become the most important thing in the world.

"I think I'll have a smoke now, and paddle over towards the lodge and see if the beavers are getting curious yet. That otter is a pretty cool customer, eating his lunch on the log right in front of me like that. Oh, look! He's pooped on it too. Leaving his mark, I guess."

Which is exactly what Ningik had just done. And he watched as the Human now did an odd thing. It took another dark little stick with a round end out of its pocket. It did something to the round end, and then made some sunlight happen in its paw, and the round end of the little stick began to make smoke. Ningik had seen smoke coming from sticks on the ground when Humans were around, and he was not afraid of it, well, not really. But he had never seen such a thing as this.

"I really must go back and try to get Ahmek out here," he thought. "Ahmek should see this. This is funny. But, of course, Ahmek doesn't have much of a sense of humour. Beavers don't. But wouldn't he find *this* funny?"

Now, Ningik was wrong about beavers and their sense of humour. There's a good reason for this. Beavers and otters don't get along together very well. So even though Ahmek and Ningik were very close friends, they knew their parents did not like them hanging around together all the time. And their friendship was quite new. So for now, they were pretty serious when they were together. And Ningik had never been with the family when they were laughing and joking, which beavers do quite a lot, as we shall soon see.

Ningik set out towards the lodge, swimming easily on the surface. Tom Thomson saw this and nodded to himself. He slid the canoe quietly into the water again. He stepped into the canoe and gave a couple of knowing twists to the paddle blade, aiming the boat towards the lodge at the far end of the pond. But moving ever so slowly.

THREE   *Steel Jaws*

N'Okomis was not interested in getting close to the Human. She surfaced near the lodge and watched the Human from a distance for a while on the shore, and then headed towards the downstream end of the pond to make sure the dam was all right. Although this was the first Human she had actually seen for herself, she knew that when there were Humans around, it was time to worry about the dam. That was Beaver Lore.

The dam seemed all right. There was no trickle over the top. It was an old dam. It had been broken and repaired many times, but it was stout and well-designed. Enough water seeped through its walls to keep the level of the pond just right, but none flowed over the top. N'Okomis sighed. An old lady should not have to do this kind of work. She ambled down the bank, on the downstream side of the dam, towards where some tender young plants looked especially tasty. This was a very old part of the dam. She could not remember ever visiting it right here, she thought. It was not far from where the break had been found when Ahmek's mother had disappeared.

The dam itself had been there long before N'Okomis was born. Her ancestors had built it, she believed. But these young plants were a new kind, she thought, and very tempting. She did not notice a few rusty links of chain that lay across the path she was taking towards the plants. The chain was very old, embedded in bark and moss. N'Okomis stepped in some soft, rotting sticks. There was something odd beneath them. She felt it and considered moving back. But it was too late. There was a loud clanging snap. Rusted steel teeth sprang up out of the mud where they had lain hidden for a long time. They closed around N'Okomis's hind leg like the jaws of a wolf.

"EEE!" she cried out. She rolled and thrashed in vain, trying to shake off the trap.

With her forepaws she grasped at a big log to try tugging herself from the jaws. But instead, the log pulled away from the wall of the dam. It loosened a heavy boulder that years before had broken from the rocks above the dam and would have tumbled to the stream below but for the heavy old log that N'Okomis had tugged on. The log had barely held the rock in place for years. Now she had upset the balance.

The stone crashed into her shoulder with a numbing blow, pinning her to the earth. N'Okomis was dizzy and out of breath. And she could not move.

She could feel blood oozing from her leg where the teeth held her. "I must rest," she thought, only half-conscious.

⚜

The man in the canoe heard the sound of a trap springing, the yelp of pain, the thrashing sound, the thump of a falling rock. He turned his canoe towards the dam.

⚜

Inside the lodge N'Osse woke up. "Where is N'Okomis? It's been too long!"

⚜

Faint as she was, the old beaver hissed a warning at Tom Thomson as he stooped over her. She could not move, but she could bare her teeth.

"Easy, old-timer," the man said. He knelt and reached towards the trap. N'Okomis's courage was stronger than her fear. She hissed and growled and struggled to free herself.

The man reached forward cautiously. He lifted the trap. Bringing out a long knife, he slipped the blade between the jaws of the trap and pried them open. He freed the bleeding leg and felt the bone in the numb and nerveless leg beneath the wound.

"Nothing broken," he said softly. "You'll be okay."

Terrified as she was, N'Okomis saw that this

was strange behaviour for a Human. Monsters are not expected to be kind.

Tom stood well back from the beaver where she was pinned beneath the rock. He made sure his foothold was safe. He picked up the heavy log that had done the damage and poked one end of it under the middle of the boulder. He heaved. The rock lifted part of its weight from N'Okomis's shoulder. She strained and wriggled free. She stared, puzzled, at the Human.

"All right, old-timer. You'll be all right," he said softly.

She did not, of course, understand the words. But there was something about the manner. She worked her way painfully to the top of the dam. Just before she dropped over the top into the water of Wiyaunuk she looked back at the Human. It had not moved. Their eyes met.

$$\text{\small 山}$$

On the lower edge of the lodge Ahmek and his father were about to slip into the water and go searching, when the water heaved in the plunge hole. N'Okomis rolled her old bulk out of the hole and fell flat on the ledge and stared at her astonished family. She looked terrible. N'Osse began to lick the cut on her foot. Ahmek nuzzled and mewed at her. What had happened? They waited for her to speak.

N'Osse glared at Ahmek as if it were all his fault. The old grandmother saw this. She sat up and said, "No. No, it is not what you think. And . . . well, Ahmek may be right about this Human, after all.

"But now," she said, " I am very tired and I hurt all

over, and I think I better have a little sleep. And then I'll tell you all about it."

ᑫᑫ

N'Okomis rolled over and yawned and rubbed her eyes and sat up in bed. "Well," she said. "Well." She yawned again and went slowly to the food store at the edge of the drying level. She sniffed at some fresh, crisp lily roots that N'Osse had brought in while she slept, smacked her lips, munched greedily for a moment, closed her eyes and nodded approval and satisfaction, and then came back into the middle of the room.

She kept them waiting while she finished chewing and swallowing. Then she told her story. Ahmek came to a terrible understanding of what must have happened to his mother so long ago. Ahmek and N'Osse didn't know what to say. That was all right, because N'Okomis had plenty to say.

She began, "Well, I have taken counsel with myself, and I have dreamed a dream. Now, my dream is a good dream. We will go quietly to the surface, the three of us, and we will watch and learn, and see if this . . . this Human . . . is to be our friend or our enemy. That is my dream."

Ahmek was amazed to hear N'Okomis use the word "friend" about a Human. But a dream was a dream; you paid attention to a dream. And N'Okomis was very firm and decisive now. Stiff and sore in her leg and shoulder, she was also wide awake and very spry for an old lady who not long before had been close to death.

And she had said the Human might be a friend!

Ahmek was feeling pleased with himself; his judgment had been good.

N'Okomis now instructed the other two beavers very clearly. N'Osse was to go to the south side of the pond, Ahmek to the northwest, she herself to the northeast (where the best poplar twigs were to be found, by the way). They were to come to the surface, just their eyes and noses, and watch quietly. "See how you *feel* about this Human," N'Okomis said. "Dream a little as you watch. Be careful, don't make a sound. But see how you feel. Then we will confer and we will know what to do."

The three beavers slipped quietly into the tunnel, N'Okomis first, then Ahmek, then N'Osse. When they came out together near the bottom of Wiyaunuk, and looked up, they were surprised. The Human's grey log was right overhead, about its own length away from the lodge, not moving. A head was projecting out from the side of the log. The head seemed to be hanging right over them, staring down. The beavers swirled around each other in a circle, then stopped and looked at each other. Ahmek waited for a sign from N'Okomis. Should they go back in?

N'Okomis nodded at her son and grandson, to encourage them to carry out her instructions anyway. So they all three headed off to their agreed positions.

When Ahmek came up near some water lilies on the northwest side, he could tell that his father was already in position at the south. He scanned the northeast side for N'Okomis. Sure enough, she was right at the shore, nibbling a poplar twig. Then she submerged out of sight for a moment, to reappear a few seconds later in the exact position she had assigned herself.

Three pairs of dark eyes, just above the still, pol-
ished surface of Wiyaunuk, now gazed at the Human in
his grey log, and tried to see it clearly, and feel something about it. And dream at the same time, in order to
know what it all meant.

ᐊᐦ

Some minutes earlier, when Tom Thomson had brought
his canoe close to the lodge, he silently stopped so that
it floated as still as a real log. He listened intently and
stared down into the black water. He could hear the
faint rustling sounds of movement inside the lodge and
what sounded like a munching sound, like somebody
biting into a crisp apple.

He kept perfectly still.

He heard the soft murmurs and whimperings of
beaver talk, inside the lodge. "They'll be coming out for
a look-see soon," he thought to himself and leaned over
the gunwale of the canoe to watch for dark shapes
emerging below.

There was silence. Then, sure enough, there was a
dip and surge of the water above the tunnel entrance.
Not far below the surface he saw a form shoot from the
opening like a torpedo from a launching tube, bursting
out with such force that the water above heaved and
dipped. One dark form, then another, then another.

Three beavers! Good. A family, he thought. They
swam slowly in a circle. They seemed to be conferring.
They were still for a moment. He blinked. They were
gone.

"Hum," Tom Thomson said to himself, disappointed. But he kept very still, all the same. He pursed his lips and, with his tongue on the roof of his mouth, began to make a sucking sound. *Shleeuourp, shleeuourp.* From their watchposts the beavers could hear what sounded like the munching of lily roots. Ahmek's mouth began to water. He could see his grandmother staring with great interest. Soon she moved. At a steady five knots, she cruised straight towards the Human in his grey log. She left a clean, undeviating wake. Halfway across she stopped and watched.

Tom Thomson pursed his lips and went *shleeuourp.*

Then, plop! He dropped something round in the water. It floated. Round and red and green. Then another, and another.

In the water three exquisitely sensitive noses began to twitch. A keen, pungent, fruity aroma came floating over the water, floating on top of the familiar scents of green algae and poplar and marsh gas bubbling from the bottom. Three sets of salivary glands began to flow.

N'Okomis now turned left and swam for ten or twelve body lengths and then dived quietly. She surfaced going the opposite way, then swam to the right, watching the Human first out of this eye and then out of that eye. She stopped.

Ahmek found the scent of those round things pretty attractive. He could not hold himself back. As he steered out into the middle of the pond he saw his father's wake there too, off to his right. Soon Tom Thomson saw three pairs of dark eyes staring at him solemnly from about a canoe-length away, and staring at the apples too, that was clear.

N'Okomis swam back and forth once more, diving silently at each reversal of her track, doing her turns submerged.

"My dream tells me that the round things in the water are — probably — good to eat," she said, surfacing beside her grandson. She spoke a bit thickly as her mouth was full of saliva. "And as I am the elder wise one . . ."

Here she sighed a sigh of great responsibility.

". . . I suppose it has fallen upon me to go there and to bite into one and see if my dream is true."

Ahmek made a thought at her: *I am willing to make the test.* But it seemed that her thought-hearing was turned off just then; she was already moving, slowly, towards the canoe. Her two hind feet gave a push in the water and stopped; she drifted cautiously towards the apples, her mouth working rather quickly.

Shleeuourp, shleeuourp, went the Human.

N'Okomis swam by the apples to the right, then to the left. Slowly she approached one and touched it with her forehead. She paused only a second, then took the apple and submerged quickly. Underwater, the furred flap inside her mouth closed to keep water from coming into her throat, and she bit hard into the fruit.

Presently she surfaced again. Her eyes darted back and forth between Ahmek and N'Osse. The apple had vanished. "I think I had better try one more, just to be sure they are safe," she said wetly.

Throughout the rest of that day the beavers came and

went, visiting with Tom Thomson, closer and closer each time. There were more apples. As the day wore on and the slanting light through the swamp spruces became flatter and redder, Tom sat calmly contemplating his painting on the easel and smoked another pipe.

Ahmek floated not far from shore with Ningik the Otter; side by side they watched the Human smoke and contemplate.

Ahmek said, "The Round Ones the Human put in the water are sweeter than water lily roots and softer than the youngest twigs. It is too bad you are a meat-eater."

Then Ahmek felt sorry for what he had said. It was a troublesome question, the meat-eating. N'Okomis had said once, "You should not really be playing with this animal. The otters are our enemies, you know. This one may act like your friend, but there is a deep need inside him to eat you. *Gooskee!* You must be watchful!

"If he had his tribe with him, we would have trouble," she said. "Now, because he is alone, it may be all right. But you must be watchful all the same."

Resentfully, Ahmek told Ningik about this. "You do not eat your friends," was all that Ningik said.

Beavers and otters, natural enemies! Both of them knew there was a truth here, a strange dark force they must watch out for; but for now, their friendship was their daily life. And today the strange and wonderful doings of the Human on the shore fascinated them and gave them something to do together.

It was the dusking light, the time when beavers are usually out of doors, swimming, eating, playing. If you go to a beaver pond when the sun is just setting, say about 8:30 of a summer evening, and if you sit silently and not too close, within minutes you will see a clean line of ripple cutting the water. If you know how to make *shleeuourp*, *shleeuourp*, and are not impatient, that clean line may turn towards you. You will probably see a nose like a pyramid, thrust straight up above the surface to scent what you are all about. And if you do not smell too terrifying . . .

This evening the Human had made a small pile of old sticks and then put some sunlight into them, with pale little sticks that went *psst!*, and the whole pile was now smoking upwards. Now the Human was very busy around this smoking sunlight from the old dry sticks, busy with black things and shiny things that made sharp little musical noises, clang, clink, plunk, scrape.

When it got dark, Ningik said good night to Ahmek and slipped away; otters do not like the dark. Beavers like the dark. Ahmek stayed watching, alone, for some time.

Inside the lodge, N'Osse said, "I suppose he is all right, our Ahmek?"

"He is all right," N'Okomis said.

"Oh, oh, those Round Ones!" she remembered. "Oh! They tasted good. This is a funny one, this Human, with its sticks and colours. But . . ."

She sat upright, lifted her right hind leg, swept her tail around, forward, so that the flat leather of it stretched out before and beneath her like the sole of a shoe. She began to rock sideways, thinking of the taste of sweet round things. "But, oh they tasted . . ."

She began to giggle at the thought. She rocked back and forth. N'Osse began to laugh, too, his old mother's giggling made him feel like laughing so hard he would fall over with rocking back and forth. Beavers often laugh so hard they fall down. They seem to like this a lot. It felt good to have had the morning's fear of human scent washed away by the taste of something sweet and the affection that came with it. Now N'Okomis actually did fall over with her laughing. Then N'Osse fell over laughing, too. They laughed and laughed. If Ningik had seen them, he would have been astonished at all this hilarity.

In the water Ahmek could hear faint sounds of laughter from the lodge. So they were not worrying, not waiting for him. He came closer to the bank and half emerged, staring at the Human and at the sunlight smoking from the pile of dry sticks. The Human was eating something. Firelight gleamed in reflection from Ahmek's dark round eyes and caught the Human's attention. He really wanted more round things, Ahmek did, but the Human made no move. After a while Ahmek became very impatient. He sat up straight on the bank and in a loud scolding trill demanded Round Ones.

"You have had enough today," Tom Thomson said quietly. Ahmek blinked and watched. The man turned and came a little closer. Ahmek thought, "This seems to be all right." Tom contemplated the beaver.

He said, "Did you know you had a four-hundred-pound ancestor in the Pleistocene? Did you know your picture is in the Pyramids? Or somewhere in Old Egypt? I have heard that, anyway. You are a very old citizen, young Ahmek.

"Did you know why your people are called the Ahmikook?" Ahmek blinked. Tom said, "It's because

this is Algonquin Territory. Ojibway country. It's been
for thousands of years. Ahmikook's the Ojibway word
for beavers. I think you beavers took from the spirit of
the Ojibway people, just as they took from you.

"Of course," he added, "you are a much better
hydraulic engineer than most people. Did you know
that?"

Ahmek liked the sound: the soft, baritone words. He
offered some muttered sounds, in return. The man
said, "That's right, young Ahmek. That's exactly right."

FOUR   *Black Canoes*

There came a day when things changed quite a lot in
Wiyaunuk.

One morning there were two more floating logs in
the pond, black logs with Humans in them. Ahmek saw
them and went back into the lodge to report.

"Perhaps there will be more Round Ones," N'Okomis
said, more to herself than anyone else, and began to
rock and giggle a little. She was combing herself with
her claws. She sat with her tail forward between her
legs and reached down to the pouches between her legs
and oiled her claws with the thick yellow oil she found
there and drew them slowly down through her long,
shiny, greying fur.

"Oh, ho, ho, ho, more Round Ones!" she chuckled,
rocking slightly, sideways, as she preened. Ahmek
blinked and he and N'Osse waited. When N'Okomis

was finally finished her grooming they all slid down to the lower level of the chamber, to the edge of the outer plunge hole, and the elders indicated to Ahmek that he should go first. He slipped quietly into the dark waters of Wiyaunuk and turned back for a moment, to watch his father and grandmother come out. N'Osse shot from the hole like a projectile, and a minor tidal wave washed over Ahmek, rippling his fur. "Someday soon," he thought, "I'll be able to do it like that." Then the huge bulk of the old lady came blasting out of the hole like a ballistic missile. "Or like *that!*" thought Ahmek admiringly. "A lifetime of practice."

The three beavers swam together towards the flat place on the bank of the pond where the friendly Human was staying. Now they saw the change. It did not feel quite right. Two dark logs were pulled partway up on the bank. Four strange Humans were talking with the beavers' friend.

The Ahmikook could not smell any Round Ones.

There was a smaller animal with the four new Humans, a four-legged animal that was like Kahminik the Wolf but a little smaller. But bigger than Waagosh the Fox. A sour, unhappy scent. One of the strange Humans spoke sharply to this animal and struck it. The animal sat down sullenly. Ahmek wondered why it did not run away.

Whereupon N'Okomis whispered, "Now here is my counsel. We will leave these new Humans . . . who have no Round Ones and who do not appear to be friendly to furred animals. We will leave them to talk with our Friend, and we will go by the canal to the West Zaudeek and eat some nice young poplar shoots. Later we will come back and see what is happening. I think that when our Friend wants to see us he will make *shleeuourp*. That is my dream just now.

"Perhaps," she added thoughtfully, "perhaps it would be a nice time to have a little sleep after we eat."

The canal was almost wide enough for two of them to swim side by side and deep enough that their paddling webbed hind feet just cleared bottom. Ahmek was always pleased at the way in which his bow waves swept the edges of the canal as he swam along; those waves seemed to announce that he was coming, that An Important Beaver was coming.

N'Okomis had said that her father or her grandfather — she was not quite sure which — had dug this canal in the old time. It still had to be dredged regularly to keep it open. Ahmek and his father would dig mud from its bottom and carry the mud back to the lodge to plaster its walls, or to Okwanim to reinforce the dam's stout structure, or to make territorial mud pats at strategic points around the pond, markers that they scented with yellow oil from their oil pouches.

The canal led west, almost sixty yards to the edge of a very old pond the beavers called West Zaudeek. It wasn't really a pond any more but a meadow. There was still a fine grove of poplars at its edge though, some big enough to provide strong logs for repairing Okwanim or the lodge. The Ahmikook would fell one of the larger trees, then cut it into short pieces, about twice their own body length, and push them down the canal with their foreheads like tugboats pushing Hudson River barges. N'Okomis's old grey head had very little fur left in the midline just above her eyes —

and even some leathery scar tissue — from pushing
heavy logs.

As they blinked in the fine morning sunlight and
nibbled tranquilly on the youngest poplars and the
fragrant grasses of the meadow, they could hear voices
at Wiyaunuk. The voices were getting louder and a
bit sharp.

"I think I had better have a little sleep here in the
sunlight," N'Okomis said, belching softly. "I am full
now, but also I think I had better have a dream about
those voices. There is something . . ."

She did not finish. Already she was on her back, her
forepaws folded on her belly, snoring softly.

Ahmek and his father lay side by side on what
was left of some fragrant royal ferns they had been
nibbling. They blinked as the harsh sounds of louder
voices drifted up from Wiyaunuk.

ᒥᑫ

"Wal, that's what we're gonna do, Mister, and you ain't
gonna stop us!"

Tom Thomson said, "Look, I've spent three days
making friends with these animals. If you have to take
beaver go up to Joe Lake, for heaven's sake. The swamps
up there are teeming with beaver. I would really appre-
ciate it if you'd hump off and let me get on with my
painting here, and leave me alone with my friends."

The men looked at him contemptuously.

"What's these here stupid things, anyway?" one
asked. He pushed at the easel. It almost fell. Tom
grabbed it just in time. He went white.

"Look here!" he said. He reached for his hatchet.

The four men ringed him, stiff, menacing. Tom tried to stare them down. The one who had done most of the talking smiled a very unpleasant smile.

"Ya better drop that thing," he said coldly.

Tom looked down at the hatchet and felt stupid for having picked it up in the first place. Suddenly his vision exploded as a fist landed in the middle of his face. He fell heavily to the ground. Someone kicked him in the ribs.

"You kin getcher canoe an get outta here, now. Or you kin stay and take what we got," the man said.

Tom breathed heavily for a while, on the ground, his face smarting with the blow. He knew there was no point in heroics. He said, "All right, all right. Give me five minutes to pack my stuff."

The man said, "Hell with that. You outta here now or you in trouble, Mister."

He laughed a dry laugh. "Unless your smelly friends with the flat tails gonna help you out."

Tom got unsteadily to his feet, hesitating.

"Now!" the man shouted. "Now!" He grabbed Tom's hatchet and flung it in the pond. Then the easel and its painting, splash! The other men came at Tom with their fists up.

Trying to keep some dignity, Tom backed to his canoe as fast as he could. He swung it onto his shoulders and headed for the trail to Canoe Lake. The man shouted after him.

"You better not say nothin' to them Park Rangers, neither," he called. *"Or we'll find you.* You got that?"

Tom plunged down the trail. His heart was heavy.

He feared for his flat-tailed friends.

♨

When the Ahmikook awoke from their nap they began
to groom each other. Out of the corner of his eye Ahmek
saw a small brown head lift out of the canal. He left
N'Osse and N'Okomis to their grooming. They did not
like Ningik, of course. But Ahmek was sure the otter
would have news.

"There are some very bad Humans at the pond,"
Ningik said. "They have fought with the friendly
Human. They threw his coloured woods and his bright
shiny things in the water and they made him take his
big log and run away. And now they have made smoke on
the shore and it looks as though they are going to stay.

"And," he added, dramatically, "they have been
crawling around on Okwanim!"

FIVE   *Bad Medicine*

"There is some very bad medicine," N'Okomis said sadly, when Ahmek recounted the otter's story. "Very bad. The worst. We will stay here at West Zaudeek until the moon is up. Then we will go back by canal, but very quietly."

They could hear nothing from Wiyaunuk, but they were sure the strangers were still there. Ahmek said, "I made a new plunge hole here on the west side a few days ago. I was going to show it to you today. We could go back that way."

In the summertime, when food is abundant and there is little building or repairs to attend to, young beavers try out their instinctive talents on a number of projects. One of them is the digging of short tunnels whose entrances look very much like groundhog holes in the forest floor, six or eight yards away from the shore, and whose exits are discreetly underwater in the bank of the pond. These tunnels are a safe way to return to the water when danger threatens on land.

N'Okomis said that, yes, they might use the new plunge hole, or they might use the canal, but they would wait until dark. And she would now eat a few of those nice royal ferns. And then perhaps have a little nap.

Ahmek wandered off upslope towards the high rocks above the poplar meadow. He found a few mushrooms to nibble on. He basked in the sun for a while, then slept under a rocky ledge, and came back to the meadow as the sun was setting.

"I think," N'Okomis said, "I think we will not wait for the moon. We will go by canal." So they did that. Ahmek was allowed to lead.

The four men had kept a fire going on the shore. They were sitting around it, laughing and drinking out of a bottle, which they passed around.

Ahmek submerged as soon as he felt the canal's water deepen beneath him at the edge of Wiyaunuk. In a moment they were all filing silently into the lodge through the safety tunnel on the shore side, not talking, not mewing, not making a sound.

In the middle of the night Ahmek awoke from a dream that told him something was amiss. A trace of moonlight gleamed at the vent in the dome of the lodge, rimming the mud-packed roof and glinting on some of the twigs and grass that hung down from the roof.

The moon was not yet high enough for the light to reach the floor, but there was some light reflecting downwards. When Ahmek walked slowly from his bed and peered towards the plunge holes he got a shock.

There was no water there! Now he could faintly hear
a rushing sound, coming through the depths of
Wiyaunuk. He felt a shiver, a warning.

His father was deep asleep, on his back, snoring.
N'Okomis was curled on her side, very still. Should
he wake them? But it was his job to investigate these
noises. This time he would go first to Okwanim, whatever else was happening. He paused at the rim of the
outer plunge hole looking down into the darkness, then
slid down into it. The water was a good half body length
below its usual level. This is bad, Ahmek thought. He
turned swiftly towards the dam. The rushing sound
grew in his ears as he swam.

Something cautioned him to surface before he came
close to Okwanim. He came up holding his nose high to
pick up scents and to turn quickly and survey on all
sides. At the far side of the pond, where the Humans
were, there was only a dull red spark left in the circle
of stones. He could see no movement. But behind him
the rushing sound was very loud. When he turned, the
moonlight reflected strongly from a hollow dip in the
water where it sluiced through a breach in the dam.
The scent of the bad Humans was very strong. Ahmek
could smell that wolf-like animal too; a fear-and-anger
smell.

"Bad medicine, all right," he said to himself, and
slipped silently beneath the surface again, right down
to the bottom where he struck out straight and certain
for the lodge, his two broad paddles working alter-
nately, push, push, for speed.

"If we wait until morning," he told N'Osse and
N'Okomis, after waking them, "there will be no water

left in Wiyaunuk. That is my thought. The water is pouring out."

N'Okomis said, "My dream tells me we should wait, that it is not safe to start work on Okwanim now."

"But we *can't* wait!" Ahmek burst out. N'Okomis darted a sharp glance at him. Ahmek said, "N'Okomis, you are wise and I think you are right, it is not safe. But if we wait until the day comes, there will be no safety at all because there will be no water."

For a beaver there is one Great Lesson that overrides all the other Great Lessons: *The water comes first.* But still N'Okomis hesitated. Her dream had been of very bad medicine. Then a dreadful sound broke the spell of her uncertainty. It was the sound of lapping water and the outside sound of crickets . . . *coming up the plunge hole!* And with a rush of cool night air. From below! Once more, N'Okomis had to agree that Ahmek was right: The Human had been friendly; now it was time to move.

Part of the way towards Okwanim they were walking on the wet bottom — that is how far the water had dropped. Just before the dam there was a kind of sink, a deep natural furrow or hollow where the old stream had eddied years before, before the beavers, before any dam, a basin scoured away by centuries of running water. The Ahmikook huddled grievously in this basin, their eyes and noses barely out of the water, watching the torrent that sluiced through the break in Okwanim, carrying away more mud and sticks every minute, slicing down through the brave old fabric of their dam, their rampart, their wall of safety from all evil.

It was time for the father to take charge, the master

builder. "First we will need some heavy logs," N'Osse said. There was a cache of them at the north side of the dam. They swam quickly to the bank, climbed out, and began to push logs down the muddy slope (where once there had been four feet of water) towards the small but deep pond that remained just at the edge of the breach in the dam.

Suddenly there was a rush of animal feet and a staccato tattoo of shrill barking sounds. A black shape leapt up over the back of the dam and threw itself at Ahmek, its teeth bared. The young beaver rolled to one side. The dog's hind claws came up and caught him over the head, slashing one of his ears. Quick as light the dog turned and squared off, crouching, its muzzle almost on the ground, its red eyes flashing at Ahmek. Nobody moved. Ahmek began a deep rumble in his throat and showed his long, sharp orange teeth.

They were on the side of the dam, a few feet from the rushing water in the breach. Ahmek began to inch back towards the safety of the water. He sensed that N'Okomis and N'Osse were already either in the water or at its edge. As Ahmek inched backwards the dog crept forward, snarling. Ahmek breathed out a sharp hissed warning through his nostrils. He could feel his tail in the water, then one webbed hind foot. The dog was crouching lower, ready to spring.

And now Ahmek made a mistake.

He desperately wanted to know where exactly the other beavers were, and so he looked away for an instant. And at that instant the black dog sprang.

The dog's teeth went deep into the thick fur of Ahmek's shoulders. Ahmek somehow found the strength

to rear up, his full length. He arched his back towards
the safety of the water, and his weight was just enough
to tumble them over. As they tumbled Ahmek turned
his head and sank *his* teeth into the first piece of dog he
came to, which was the throat, and grasped a big fold of
loose hairy skin with his razor teeth. He sank back into
the dark water pulling his attacker under with him.

The dog thrashed and struggled, wildly trying to
swim. It let go its grip on Ahmek's fur and writhed
urgently, trying to escape the relentless power of those
orange teeth. Bubbles were coming from its nose and
mouth. Its red eyes were blinking frantically, staring in
supplication at the young beaver. But the beaver was
very sure now, very solid. He was in his element, his
strong hind legs pumping, pumping, drawing them
deeper and deeper, down into the basin.

In the thinning green moonlight, at the bottom of
the cavity, in the old stream bed below the breach that
its cruel masters had made in the dam, the dog's dimming eyes now saw another dark shape approach. A
bulky, grizzled beaver. An ancient beaver, with ancient
eyes that seemed to look right through its dimming
vision and into its brain. With a message.

You will go away now and not come back.

The dog tried to signal understanding. Its mind was
clouding, its lungs bursting.

Under the water, N'Okomis then looked into
Ahmek's dark, gleaming eyes. *You can let go now.*
Ahmek reluctantly let go. The dog thrashed its way to
the surface and scrambled up the bank. It ran screech-
ing across the west end of the dam. There was a loud
crashing noise as it slithered through heavy brush and

banged into a tree. Whimpering piteously as it ran, the dog kept on crashing through the forest until its sounds faded away.

Ahmek, his father, and his grandmother rested at the edge of the dam, their heads just out of the water. Ahmek was breathing pretty hard. His father looked at him admiringly. "My brave Ahmek," he said, after a while. N'Okomis looked at him in a new way, too, and her thoughts agreed with N'Osse.

N'Osse said, "Now we must get to work."

For half an hour they continued to push logs down the bank into the basin. Then they began to swim them across the basin towards the breach in the dam. After a moment, Ahmek realized that someone was swimming along beside them. Ningik.

Ningik whispered, "Ahmek, please stop a moment and listen to me."

Although N'Okomis and N'Osse still didn't like Ahmek and Ningik's friendship, the otter had told them the important news about the bad Humans earlier, so they kept on swimming, leaving Ahmek to talk to Ningik. Soon Ahmek caught up with them. Now they were at the bank of the dam, ready to start pushing logs into the breach.

"Stop!" Ahmek said sharply. They looked at him in surprise.

"Now I know you do not like Ningik and you do not really trust him. But he is my friend, and he told me something very important. He does not like to be out at night but while we were sleeping he heard something and came out and saw the strange Humans at Okwanim. He saw them breach the dam. He said they put some bad medicine in the breach, something hard and evil. He said we should not go there."

"Let me have a look," N'Osse said.

"No!" Ahmek cried, but N'Osse was already pushing his log towards the breach. The log struck something that rang out. There was a loud snap. A wire gate appeared out of nowhere and snapped shut over a big wire box, inches from N'Osse's head. Bang!

There was a cry from the bank where the men had their tents. "There they are! Git the boxes!" Running feet, lanterns, swinging along the shore, feet splashing in the marshy water.

Ningik was beside them. "Run away, Ahmek!" he pleaded. It seemed too late. Flashes of light were picking them out. The Humans were almost upon them. N'Okomis cried out in terror. There was splashing in all directions. Ahmek knew his father and grandmother were escaping, and he must, too, but where! He plunged. At the edge of the basin he came up, there was no more water.

"There!" He heard a sharp voice from the shore, and a flash of light came by his head.

Close by he saw the mouth of his new escape tunnel. Now it was above the waterline; there was no water. But he scampered into it anyway, and crawled partway along it towards the entrance hole in the forest floor a few yards inshore. Something told him to stop and be silent.

Loud thundering feet over his head. Sounds of cursing. Splashing feet in the marshy pond edge.

Ahmek crouched silently and waited, alert, ready to fight or run if he had to. He heard nothing. He knew he must not move. It seemed to be a very long time.

When the first light came he crept silently to the mouth
of the tunnel in the bank. He looked out. On the far side
of the now almost empty pond two Humans were
putting their black logs on their shoulders, two more
hoisting their brown lumpy shapes on their backs.
There was no sign of the four-legged animal that had
attacked him. The Humans headed down the trail north
towards Zaaghigan, the big lake. Ahmek watched till
they were gone. Then he came out on the edge of the
muddy bottom, the almost empty pond. He did not feel
safe. He eased back into shelter and waited. There was
no more sound of Humans, but it did not feel safe
outside. He dozed for a while, woke, came to the opening and looked out, but still did not feel safe about
coming out. So, although he was hungry and thirsty
and needed a bath, he stayed in his tunnel till the night
fell again.

Finally he came out and climbed up onto the shore
and looked all about. He mewed softly.

"N'Osse, my father? N'Okomis?"

Then, "Ningik?"

There was no answer, as he knew there would not
be. He went very quiet and waited for a dream to give
him direction. Something was telling him to go south.
When the moon came up, an hour later, he walked
heavily up the almost dry bed of the canal to West
Zaudeek. He ate as much grass and leaves and royal
ferns and young alder twigs as he could, to give him

strength. Somehow he knew he was about to make a long journey. He turned to say good-bye to Wiyaunuk. On a night like this there would always have been a gleam of moonlight on still water. Now there was only a dark, empty gash and the smell of mud and decaying bottom vegetation.

Although he knew that he was doing what he must do, as he turned and began to walk towards the south, he felt a sense of loss more bitter than anything that had happened in his young life since the Ningoshkauwin, the disappearance, that time when his mother had gone to repair the dam and was never seen again.

SIX

A Pale Shape Gliding

The first part of Ahmek's night journey took him unaccustomedly high, over some bare rock and from ledge to ledge among the twisted roots of thin pines hanging bravely onto the side of what was almost a cliff of ancient red granite. Some of these small trees were very old; they had been holding onto the rock for a long, long time. Their tough roots pushed for water and nourishment deep into cracks in the old rock. There was not much for them in those cracks, but they held on. The rock face ran roughly in a north-south line, so there was some moonlight on it, and Ahmek could choose the best path with little difficulty.

On this high ground grew almost nothing that beavers like to eat. There was no water at all, no streams, no pools. This did not matter to Ahmek for now. His mission was to go south. His brain was focused on south.

Beavers do not like to be alone, and so there was a sadness about that part; but there were no second thoughts, no stopping to think it over — Is-this-the-right-move? Wiyaunuk was finished, contaminated, dangerous; he would have to find a new Wiyaunuk; that was all.

Soon Ahmek was at the highest point of all. To the west the land dropped away sharply. He looked over the tops of trees. There, in the distance, was the gleam of moonlight on a big water, Zaaghigan, maybe. Ahmek lifted his nose and smelled deeply. He could smell water. As soon as he caught that scent he wanted water, wanted to be in water, to bathe and to groom himself afterwards, to dive, to drink. But he must go on south. He went on south.

Some hours passed. It was as if there was nothing else in the world but the dark invisible trail leading towards this south that he must go towards. Once a big owl cruised low, almost silently over his head, close enough for Ahmek to catch the sharp dusty scent of the great wings. The owl was looking for something to eat. Ahmek knew that once he might have been a candidate for the big bird's supper, but he was now too big for the owl; he kept straight on and did not even look up. The owl grunted and disappeared silently, navigating magically through the palisade of invisible black tree trunks.

By the time the moon had reached its highest point and had begun to descend towards the west, Ahmek had come upon lower ground and taller trees, still on a sloping bed of granite. The moon now cast long, hard shadows on the rock and on the forest floor. Ahmek plodded along without slowing, but the shadows made it harder to make out the best path. He stepped on what he thought was just a shadow on the sloping rock but turned out to be loose gravel and old dead leaves. They went slithering out from under him; he lost his footing and slid bump bump down the rock, ending up hard against an old pine stump with a knock that took his breath away.

For the first time that night he felt it would be good to stop and rest. His eyes swept around the darkening forest. He could see nothing in the shadows. He closed his eyes. He had no shelter so he would not sleep, but his eyes were dry and tired, and he let them stay closed for several minutes.

Suddenly, he sensed, rather than heard something, a soft movement, not close but not far either. He opened his eyes instantly and peered into the blackness. There! Was it a stray late moonbeam?

Something white moved in the forest, gliding smoothly, then stopping, then moving on again, stately, silent. Then it was gone. Ahmek felt the fur on his back and shoulders rise. He felt cold there, between his shoulders. He tried to catch a scent. For a strange moment he thought he smelled beaver. There was something cold in the scent. He looked up instinctively for the source of the cold, as he would have in the lodge, cold air coming in from the vent, or a break in the logs, time to fix the roof. He felt the need of a roof, of a safe, deep, dark place with a roof.

But, in fact, that cold was normal. If Ahmek hadn't felt a bit a shiver from glimpsing that . . . strange, pale shape gliding silently along, he would hardly have noticed it. It was that special cold of the early morning, which creeps over the land an hour before sunrise, when the earth has given up all its stored heat through the dark of the night. But lakes hold on to their heat much longer; they keep the air above them warm, too. So in the morning, the warmer air that hovers over the lakes begins to rise, ever so slowly, and as it rises it draws cold air down the slopes towards the water.

꒰ꙩ꒱

What Ahmek felt just then was also happening a few miles away, down at the edge of Canoe Lake, on a flat bed of rock where Tom Thomson had made his camp. He had tried to ease the swelling in his bruised nose by bathing it in cold water, and then he put his things in order, calming himself down after his encounter with those poachers. He finally dozed off in his blanket roll, under the shelter of his grey canoe. But now the cold crept under the edge of the canoe, and brushed the back of his neck. Tom woke up, poked the remains of his fire, heated up some tea, munched a crust of bread, packed his gear, and put the canoe into the water. He had promised to meet some friends that morning and still had some miles to paddle north.

The same cold air, flowing down over the muddy basin that used to be Wiyaunuk, sponged up several hundred pounds of moisture from the still steaming bed of the pond and carried it down to the lake, turning it into a dense wall of fog rolling out of the little bay in the northeast corner of the lake.

Tom Thomson saw that solid wall of fog ahead of him, as he rounded the bend just south of it. "There's an old story of a murdered Park Ranger whose ghost can be seen on a night like this," he thought.

The moon was low in the west, off to his left. He chose to keep just outside the fog bank. Paddlers have been known to go around in circles for hours, hopelessly lost in fog, all the time believing they are paddling straight ahead. Not Tom Thomson. He kept his eyes on the North Star, straight ahead, to guide him. His canoe slid along, slip, slip, went the paddle, just at the edge of the fog bank. Suddenly, just like Ahmek, he felt a shiver that was not from the cold air. There was a shape — not pale but dark — a phantom paddler, right beside him, matching him stroke for stroke, just inside the fog, its paddle not making a sound. And for a moment . . . .

Just a few miles away, up in the forest, where Ahmek had seen a pale shape and smelled something puzzling, he now caught whiff of another scent, a good scent of swamp plants and water. Although the moon was still hanging low somewhere there in the west behind the treetops, there was a pale glow in the eastern sky. Day was coming. That could be dangerous. With the first hint of dawn there was a chilling stillness. Then there was the faintest movement of rising air from the south. Ahmek could not really see much towards the south, but he sensed that the ground was lower that way, and there was a hint of water, a swampy smell like Mushkeeg back at Wiyaunuk. *Go that way.*

Another hour of walking and the sky was now quite light. This made Ahmek uneasy, although he was pretty sure that the Humans in the black logs were a long way behind him. But he wanted to sleep, and in this strange country it would not do to sleep in the open. The ground was softer now, perhaps he could dig, get some sticks, build a roof. But he kept heading down the slope towards the smell of swamp.

And good! The pines thinned out at the bottom of the slope, and Ahmek came out in an old beaver meadow. He found a stream and drank thirstily. There were ferns and water plants to eat. It was too light to linger, but he must eat something. And as he moved along the bank of the stream he stumbled happily on what his instincts had been telling him to look for all the time: an old abandoned escape hole, made long ago by beavers who had once lived here, who had once made a dam, a pond, a lodge . . . and, of course, escape tunnels.

The mouth of the escape hole was overgrown and cluttered, but Ahmek's strong forepaws and teeth cleared it out in minutes. Down below it was dry and dark. And safe!

Before Ahmek settled down to sleep in this burrow, he thrust his nose outside for a last look around the meadow. At the far side, in the pines at the bottom of the slope, where he had come out into the meadow, and where there was still deep shadow, he saw a white . . . thing!

The thing did not move. It seemed to be watching. It was too big for what its shape suggested: the shape of a beaver. And it seemed to be staring straight at Ahmek!

Ahmek glanced quickly behind him into the dark safety of his burrow. When he looked back at the forest a second later, the shape was not there.

"It is a dream," Ahmek said to himself. He found the sound of his own voice comforting. "It is a dream, but I don't understand what it is trying to tell me."

"Ah well," he mewed, "maybe it will speak more clearly in my sleep."

But he was, well, a little bit scared. And even though he worked his way a long distance down the abandoned burrow, where it was silent and surely very safe, it took him awhile to get to sleep.

♆

When Ahmek awoke he was hungry. The sun was bright in the afternoon sky. The water in the stream was gurgling and laughing. Ahmek stuck his head out of the hole and then stepped out boldly and looked around. A blue jay was yelling overhead. By a cluster of cardinal flowers two hummingbirds were dive-bombing each other, squeaking and swooping. At the bank of the stream a family of rabbits looked up at him, decided that the young beaver posed no threat, and kept on nibbling. The meadow smelled of peace.

Ahmek tried to remember whether he had dreamed about the white shape, but all he could hold on to from the fleeting images of his sleep was . . . *south*. Stronger than ever. South and getting closer, the messages seemed to say.

He had a good feed of thick, juicy grasses, several flavours. He dug some cattail roots and munched them greedily. Then he had a long bath. He washed his nose carefully first. Ahmek had an especially runny nose. So did his father and his grandmother. This was a family trait. Not all beavers have runny noses, but they all start their daily cleansing by washing them, and in Ahmek's family it was specially important because of this odd runny nose they had. After he washed his nose, he drew oil from the pouches between his legs and combed his head and then his chest and his tummy and his arms, working the oil well into his shining fur. He wished N'Okomis were there to do his back. N'Okomis was not there. He did his thighs and his legs and his sides. Afterwards he sat on a flat rock in the sunlight and flipped his tail forward between his legs and carefully squeezed all the water out of his fur, as far as he could reach. Now he felt like a good beaver again.

"It would be nice to have a little nap now," he said out loud to himself, imitating the voice of N'Okomis. His imitation made him laugh and rock back and forth. He climbed the bank of the stream and headed back to the old burrow. Soon he was curled up, three feet below the floor of the meadow. He went to sleep immediately.

The sun was low and red when he came out again, and he felt full of energy and hope. An osprey swooped over the meadow, Wingizwaush, one of the Lesser Enemies. Osprey are fish hawks, but they sometimes prey upon other small swimmers, including beaver kits. "So what?" Ahmek thought, confidently. "I am too big for him now. And I'm not in the water anyway."

He struck off south across the meadow grasses, stopping occasionally to nibble a juicy stem or a fragrant marsh flower, and he mewed and hummed as he went along. This is good, this is good, something was telling him. This is a good direction.

He felt so good that about two hours after it got dark, the moon not yet in sight though there was a soft glow coming over the tops of the trees, so good that he thought it would be, well, nice to have one more little nap, just a short one. After all, he had a long night's walk ahead of him.

In fifteen minutes he had cut sticks and built a small roof against an old twisted stump, a sort of lean-to, just enough to feel right about sleeping. When they are grazing together in a meadow beavers may nap in the open. But a lone beaver, in strange territory, prefers to have something over his head when he sleeps. Ahmek stretched out on his back under his little roof and began almost immediately to snore.

Ten minutes later he opened his eyes with a start.

There was something there, just outside his little shelter, staring at him. White. A large, white beaver shape, standing on its hind legs, its wide, flat tail (also white!) tucked forward. It was big, fifty or sixty pounds if it was real, tall, staring at Ahmek with eyes that were . . . strange. Pink!

In the moonlight, its eyes were *pink*.

But it smelled like a real beaver, and it smelled friendly.

"*Wenesh Giin?* Who are you? . . . ," Ahmek began. He was still inside his shelter. Then he rocked forward and stuck his head out and looked at the big white beaver. "I was asleep," Ahmek said apologetically. "Are you by any chance my dream?"

"Ah," said the big white beaver.

Then he said, "We are such stuff as dreams are made on, you know. And our little lives are rounded with a sleep."

Ahmek blinked slowly, trying to puzzle out what *that* all meant. He said, "Some bad Humans came and broke Okwanim. There is no more water in my Wiyaunuk. I don't know where my father is, or my grandmother, either. It was pretty much the end of the world for me when the whole middle of the dam came all to pieces and washed away, so . . ."

The tall white shape listened carefully to Ahmek's tale, and nodded gravely. "Things fall apart," he said. "The centre cannot hold."

"That's right," Ahmek said eagerly. "And something told me I must go south, and I wondered . . . if . . . you . . . ."

The white beaver did not say anything, but he looked kindly at Ahmek.

Ahmek felt embarrassed about this, but he went on. "And I think I saw you last night, in the forest, and again this afternoon, so I wondered . . . I mean," Ahmek said, "what . . . what are you doing here?"

"I am doomed for a certain time to walk the night," he said. "Haply, for I am white, you see, they did not want me in the lodge. Or in the pond or in the swamp, or anywhere, it seems, as far as I can tell. They pushed me away, as if I were not a proper beaver."

Ahmek thought about this. "It is true that all the beavers I've ever seen were brown or black. I'm brown and my head is black. My father says that is unusual. But you *are* a beaver, aren't you? You're not a dream," Ahmek said disappointedly.

"Have you ever seen a dream walking?" his new acquaintance asked. "Well I have." He hummed a little melody, and then sighed. "But," he said more seriously, "I may be a dream, too. There are more things in heaven and earth than are dreamt of in your philosophy, Horatio. I have had a very strange life. Perhaps I shall tell you about it sometime, or perhaps not. But I have learned some wise things. And I know a lot about Humans."

He looked deep into Ahmek's eyes. "You would be called Ahmek, I believe," he said. It seemed right, to Ahmek, that the stranger would know his name. Not Horatio, he was glad to hear.

"So, what is your name?" Ahmek asked.

"Well, why don't you call me Mudjeekawis? I would like you to remember me as a kind of . . . elder brother. I did not have any younger brothers, and you may, or, well, you might . . . ."

Now Mudjeekawis began to look a bit embarrassed. Ahmek understood this. He said kindly, "Well, I think that would be fine, but I think that I have to keep on going south now. *Bizhaun?* Will you come with me?"

"I am not allowed to do that," said Mudjeekawis. "But you will see me again. Now attend carefully, young Ahmek, for I am going to give you a Message. And then you will go your way, and I will go a different way. And you must not look back, after me. But you will see me again. *Giin bizhaun.* Come here."

It was not words that Mudjeekawis gave to Ahmek then. When beavers want to give each other a really important message, a message beyond words, they stand close together, on their hind feet, and put their

forepaws on each other's shoulders. They put their
heads together and push at each other. Humans say the
beavers are wrestling, or dancing, when they do this.
Sometimes indeed they are only wrestling or dancing.
But often what they are doing is something that
humans do not know how to do. Perhaps we did once,
but not any more.

As Ahmek held onto Mudjeekawis and their heads
touched, the young beaver entered a wide, comforting
space. It flowed into his knowing from the big white
beaver. There was an eagerness in the air of the space.
Beneath the space was water, a Wiyaunuk almost
certainly, and in the space and in the water was a
greeting and a certainty; he would *know* this space
when he came to it, this water. Mudjeekawis had given
him a picture of it. He would feel a greeting there: the
Message.

There was something else, a Not-Loneliness, in this
space, this water.

And then it was over. Ahmek and the big white
beaver were, for a moment, just dancing and wrestling
after all. The Message had passed. They were touching
and laughing a little in their throats, darker sounds
than mewing, good sounds. And then they pushed off,
and Mudjeekawis nodded, *turn now*. Ahmek turned. He
saw that the moon was just edging up over the trees.
That gave him his direction. He managed — it wasn't
easy — not to turn around for another look back at his
new friend and teacher. He took up his journey to the
south once more. His whole spirit was singing.
Something wonderful was going to happen, that was
for sure.

SEVEN   *Meanwhile*

Ahmek's trail south through the thick forest had
taken him at first parallel to the east shore of
the big water, Zaaghigan, which lay just west of his
old pond, Wiyaunuk. Wiyaunuk's stream ran into
Zaaghigan. This big water is called Canoe Lake. A few
days' beaver travel north of where Ahmek had spent
the night (but only a few hours by canoe for humans
paddling up Canoe Lake) there is an old concrete dam
and a waterfall where the waters of another big lake
fall into Canoe Lake. This other lake is called Joe Lake.
You can go and see both lakes today; the dam and the
falls have scarcely changed since Ahmek's time. If it
is summertime when you walk the narrow path past
the dam, you may have to step aside every few minutes
to let pass the fifty to a hundred canoe-trippers who
portage there almost every day in July and August. The

old railway tracks that used to bring the summer visitors and take out the lumber have been removed, but the road bed can still be seen snaking through the forest and around the south shore of Joe Lake.

At Wiyaunuk, Ahmek and his family had sometimes been awakened from a morning nap by the sound of a great thunder coming from the direction of Joe Lake. Sensitive to the motions and the slightest tremblings of the earth and the water, they could feel a deep rumbling in the ground when this thunder spirit passed. It was a rhythmic, beating thunder, not like those grand, chaotic, disorderly, terrifying thunders that come when the sky grows dark and is split wide open by jagged lines of light and rain pelting down. This other thunder beat faster than Ahmek's heart when he had been swimming hard underwater. It was often accompanied by a great wailing song, *whooo-ooo, whooo-oo*.

Ahmek used to wonder if this unnatural thunder was the Wendigo or some other evil spirit. The Wendigo, as he understood it, lived at the bottom of big waters and could cause dreadful things to happen. He had asked his dreams if this big thunder was the Wendigo, but there had come no answer. Often the thunder would grow slower in its heartbeats, and then fade and stop for a while, and then start up again.

As Ahmek had begun to make his way towards the powerful south that was calling him, he became dimly aware that the Wendigo sound was getting fainter and fainter the farther south he went.

Once, as he was going off to sleep, some trick of wind direction, or clouds that can reflect sound back from the sky, brought that thunder spirit right into the beginning of his dream. In it he saw his mother, Silvertips. She was floating in a black, black river made of thunder spirit. She was terrified in the dream, and so was Ahmek. It was a strong and a terrible nightmare, and when he woke again he lay shivering for a long time before the image left him.

On the very morning that Ahmek was plodding doggedly towards his destiny, the thunder spirit rolled and clanked noisily into Joe Lake station, before dawn, and stopped there. Some men got off. One of the men carried a painter's sketch box, stained with old colours and dark with oil. Another gingerly lifted down a big black camera on a tripod. The camera was covered with a large black cloth. A third man busied himself at the baggage car, carefully taking off a brand-new, bright red, canvas-covered canoe.

The one with the sketch box strolled down to the shore. The morning mist hung low over the lake in the first streaks of light in the east. On the beach was another canoe, a grey one, pulled well up on the sand. On his knees beside the grey canoe, a tanned, lean, fit-looking man was busy repacking his gear in a compact set of three small packsacks plus a small wooden box. He carefully arranged some small painted wooden panels to fit them into slots in the lid of his wooden box, so that the wet paint would not rub off, and the panels would be safe for travel.

The first passenger from the train saw this fellow

and looked back at his friends who were now bringing the red canoe towards the water. He pointed silently at the man on his knees with his back to them.

The three men smiled at each other and came up behind Tom Thomson silently. Tom pretended to be so absorbed with his packing that he didn't hear them at all.

Until one of them called out "BOO!" in a loud voice, and Tom turned calmly, looked up at them, and smiled.

"Hello, Alex," he said, "I thought that might be you. Hello, Lawren. Hello, Jim. I've a fire laid over there on the rock, ready to make you tea, and then I'll point you in the direction I think you should go, and you can get started."

Alex Jackson said, "Well now, Lawren and Jim and I were hoping you'd come with us."

Tom said, "Alex, you know your way around this park as well as I do. I just thought I would suggest some territory you should see this time of the year, and then I think I'll head up into the hills on my own. Maybe we can meet back here at the end of the week."

Lawren Harris looked over Tom's shoulders at one of the paintings in the slotted lid of the box.

"Why that's very fine work, Tom!" he said. "You've really caught the spirit of this wonderful land. But I've never seen you paint an animal before."

He pointed at a strongly drawn little panel in greens and browns, with one blob of red where a swimming beaver, in a dark, calm pond, was approaching an apple that floated just in front of him.

Tom said, "Well, this little fellow and I got to know each other a bit, and he took my fancy. I'll give it to you, if you like, Lawren. Get your mind off those Toronto street scenes you're always painting."

The three men laughed, but Lawren Harris was pleased with his gift, and stowed the panel carefully in his own painting kit. Tom soon got the fire going, and before long they were squatting around the fire, or sitting on stones, blowing on the steaming brown liquid, sipping from the hot tin mugs.

Tom told his friends about portaging over the dam. He pointed them south and he warned them about the poachers in the black canoes.

Soon they all packed up. The three men in the red canoe headed south, the one in the grey canoe, north. As the bend in the river was about to separate them, they all turned and gave a long wave of farewell to each other.

EIGHT   *Wah-jusk*

Ahmek pushed steadily through a thick mess of
young spruce and tangled, bitter-smelling alder.
The going was hard but Ahmek was excited: he could
smell running water and the musky scent of beaver
grass. When he paused from time to time, to look about
him and to listen, he could hear the burbling and
shushing of a stream. Just ahead, it sounded.

There was something very special about this water;
although he could not see it, he felt it must be the same
water and the same space he had found in
Mudjeekawis's Message.

Ahmek paused and stood up straight and listened
again. He felt a bit lonely.

"Are you there, Mudjeekawis?" he mewed.

Inside him there was an answer. *Keep going.* He put
his head down and bulldozed through the tangle. He

felt the ground becoming wetter under his feet. A good place was just ahead, that was certain.

But the tangle got thicker and thicker and the going harder and harder. It was almost as if the forest did not want Ahmek to penetrate it just there, or not just yet. He had to snap and chew and tug at the wiry, thorny stems to make a passage for himself.

Presently he came out into a small clearing. To one side and to the other the land was grassy and smooth. The water was straight ahead; he could smell it and hear it. But straight ahead also lay more of that tangled undergrowth. "Well," Ahmek thought. "I'll just have to put my head down and keep on chewing my way through it."

Just then there was a rustling sound in the grass off to his left. Ahmek peered that way, quickly. He didn't see anything, but he thought the grass was moving a bit. He heard a little chuckling sound, an animal's voice. It was not a fearful voice. He waited, wondering who this might be. Ningik?

A small furry head popped up out of the grasses, tiny dark eyes laughing, a split second, and then disappeared again. The grass moved. The animal was playing a game.

Ahmek caught a scent and now he knew what kind of animal it was.

"Come on, you muskrat," he called. "I know you're there. Come out and make friends."

There was another chuckle, this time from right behind him. Ahmek turned quickly but could see nothing. The chuckle came again from the opposite side of the clearing. Ahmek whirled towards the sound,

puzzled and amused. Behind him a funny old voice
said, "Fooled ya, din't I!"

Ahmek turned back. In the grass directly opposite
and a long way from the place where the last chuckle
had sounded, there was indeed a wiry, grizzled old
muskrat standing on its hind legs and grinning mischievously at the young beaver.

"Wah-jusk," the old fellow said. "That's my name, if
you want to know. Wah-jusk. And at my age, if you can
b'lieve this, I'm learnin' to throw my voice. To fool the
other animals. Pretty good, eh? What do you say?
Bounce it off the trees. Watch!"

He ducked into the grass. Ahmek heard a chuckle
from right behind him. He whirled around despite
himself.

"Hee, hee, hee, hee, hee!" cackled the old muskrat.
"Gotcha again, din't I! Oh I am getting good at this!
I bet yer from the north up by Zaaghigan, am I right?
All them beavers up there got a snotty nose like yours,
no insult intended. What brings ya down south here,
hmm? Haven't been any beavers here for a coupla
years or so, maybe more. I know. Yer on yer wander
year, kicked outta the nest, hey? Happens to all young
beavers, don't worry. You'll be okay. Good-looking setta
teeth there. Gotta dream to guide ya? Spec' ya have.
They all have, beavers. Don't put much stock in dreams
myself, depend more on my wits. Watch this!"

He ducked into the grass again. Astoundingly,
Ahmek heard the scrabbling sound of an animal climb-
ing a tree way on the other side of the clearing. This
time he didn't turn around — he was catching on. So
when Wah-jusk popped up out of the grasses again

Ahmek was waiting for him.

"How did you do that?" Ahmek said, admiringly. "That was amazing."

"Hey, hey. I think I'm going to like you," Wah-jusk said. "I *am* pretty good fer an old fella, ain't I? Wanta play hide and seek? Ya'd never find me, ya know. I got all kindsa tricks. Well . . .," he said after a moment, "I suppose yer tryna git to the stream, are ya?"

Ahmek said, "I, I had to go south. My . . . my dream gave me a Message. And now I think, I really think, that I am about to arrive at the place where I'm . . . , well, supposed to be. Only it is very hard going, just here."

The old muskrat looked at Ahmek with half a smile on his face. "It's where I live, you know," he said. "Lived here all my days. Since I was just a kit."

He sighed. "Used to sing when I was younger," he said. "Wanna hear a good song? Well, maybe later. Hey, did I do the one with the animal scrabblin' up the tree? Oh yeah. I did. Anyway, yer a beaver after all. So I spose you'll wanna come waddlin' in here to my old meadow, chewin' and scratchin', and build one a them . . . whatsits? Dam things? Make a big dam anna pond and all that? Change my whole waya life? Is that it?"

Ahmek thought about it. It had never occurred to him that his building a dam and a pond, (which, of course, he *had* to do in order to live in safety) it had never occurred to him that this would be unwelcome to anyone else. After all, a pond was, really, there was nothing nicer in the world than a pond, and you had to have a dam to have a pond. He didn't quite know what to say.

Wah-jusk the Muskrat blinked at Ahmek for a
moment. Then he said, "Ya oughta know the story.
The first muskrat ever, Zhashkoonh? Well, see, this
Zhashkoonh, he done a great favour to Nanabush
during the flood, remember? So Nanabush said, 'I owe
ya sump'n. What part of the world would'ja like, when
the flood dries up and the land comes back?' So my old
ancestor says, 'I want the blue lakes.' 'You gottem,'
Nanabush says. Well, you know what we're like. The
old guy, this Zhashkoonh, he comes back next day, says,
'Nanabush,' he says, 'I changed my mind, I want the
grasslands.' Nanabush says, 'Mister,' he says 'Around
here we don't go for mind-changin'. Specially when I'm
busy creatin' the world just now. So ya had yer chance,
kid, and here's what I'm gonna do. What yer gonna get
is a little of each. Namely swamps. Part grassland, part
lakes.' So that's what we got, and — ya know what? We
come to like it."

The muskrat paused. "Lookit," he said after a
while. "It's been kinda lonely here since my old . . . ."
Here he choked and cleared his throat noisily, and had
to pause and collect himself.

"Well, she was my partner, ya know. And she loved
to hear me sing, too. I guess I kinda stopped singing
when she . . . . And she never did see me do that bounce
my voice offa the trees thing. Anyway, lonely here, I
said, anna bit quiet, nobody to sing to, chew the fat
with. And, well. A pond . . . ."

He was silent.

"Come to think of it," he said presently, "if we hadda
pond we'd get some cattails, hey? And some lilies and
arrow weed too, hey? You like to eat arrow weed?"

"Oh yes!" Ahmek said, and his mouth watered.

"Well, listen," said Wah-jusk the Muskrat. "Listen. I think it's time ya started buildin' a dam so we getta pond, and then them cattails can getta start, hey? Ya come along with me, here, this way, through the grass. I kin show ya an easy way down to the meadow and the stream, ya don't hafta keep chewin' yer way through them stupid alderswamps like ya was doin', long way around is the short way home, hey? Anyway, come along with me now."

And the muskrat jerked his head over his lean old grizzled shoulder to indicate the way, and together the two new friends headed off, by a circular path, still down hill, still more or less towards the south, towards the sound of running water and towards the rich, thick smell of beaver grass, which grew stronger and stronger as they went down.

NINE   *Ahmek the Builder*

W ah-jusk's meadow spread out across a narrow
valley fortified to the north and the south by high
walls of strong, pink granite topped with noble old pine
trees. Like that meadow where Ahmek had spent the
night in an abandoned safety tunnel, this valley, too,
had once been home to beavers, but not since a very
long time. Instead of an open expanse of grass there
were poplars — hundreds of them, maybe thousands,
five or six years old at least, some as broad in the trunk
as Ahmek's scaly tail.

Now poplars are among the beaver's most important food. Nothing is better for the winter food cache.
The bark is full of vitamins and the wood is soft and
easy to cut. The twigs are tasty, though not as tasty as
arrow weed or cattail roots. This meadowful of waving,
trembling poplars made Ahmek a bit homesick. It was

quite a lot like the West Zaudeek; as soon as he thought of West Zaudeek he thought of N'Okomis and N'Osse. And that was hard.

But, oh! There was more than enough wood to make a fine dam, and there was a bright gentle stream that rippled along one side of the meadow until, with a gurgle and rush, it tumbled over a ledge of rock and down onto lower, rocky ground thick in cedar and black spruce. The sound of the water tumbling through the notch in the ledge made Ahmek's forepaws twitch.

There is something about the sound of running water that makes a beaver want to build. All beavers, all over the beaver world, from Sweden to California, from Seattle to Antigonish, can simply not prevent themselves from building when they hear the sound of running water. If you put beaver in a zoo — which it is hoped you will never be cruel enough to do (besides, it is easy to go and visit beavers in the wild, so why bother with a zoo?) — well, anyway, if you do, and you want to get them started building something that looks like a dam, just give them lots of poplar saplings and then turn on a tap or even play a recording of rushing water. The beavers will start to build. They can't help it. Any more than you can probably help eating salted peanuts.

While Wah-jusk the Muskrat had been counting on a little companionship, someone to show off his voice-throwing to and play jokes on and maybe even sing to, he was going to have to wait. Ahmek had been bewitched, captivated, enchanted, entranced, rapt, seized, spellbound. The whole world had disappeared except for a gap in a rocky ledge and a rushing stream and an endless supply of young, succulent, quivering poplars.

Anyone who has not seen a beaver at work when the building fit has hit would not believe what happened next. Ahmek did not stop to sleep. He forgot about Wah-jusk. He forgot about the mysterious white beaver in the night, about his father, about his grandmother, even about Wiyaunuk. His whole being was filled with an eagerness to bite wood and dig mud and build dam. So that's what he did.

First he tilted his head sideways at the base of a fine young poplar that stood only a treetrunk's length away from the place where the water flowed over the ledge. His powerful orange teeth took two long chips out of one side, as long as half his tail. Then he bent the other way and two more long strips fell from the opposite side of the tree. Then back to the first side and two more, then two more. In less time than it takes to read this page, the poplar swayed and crashed down. Unfortunately it fell away from the notch in the ledge where the water spilled out, not towards it. Beavers (unlike what you may have heard) have no idea which way their tree will fall. Sometimes they get conked on the head and seriously hurt by the very tree they are cutting down. This happens to humans, too, by the way.

So the first tree fell the wrong way. That did not seem to bother Ahmek. He pounced upon the trunk just above his first cut and, chop! chop! gnaw! gnaw, in a minute he had a fine short log with pointed ends. Then another and then another. And then it was time for another tree.

The wiry old muskrat sat restlessly on a stone humming snatches of some old melody, just loud enough that the beaver might hear it and ask for the whole song. He watched this display of industry with some distaste.

"Yer obsessed!" he called out once. Ahmek nodded in happy agreement, whatever that word meant, and kept on cutting wood. From time to time he sat up on his tail and caught his breath and ground his teeth against each other sideways, back and forth, to sharpen them for the task, and then without pausing to eat or drink he got back to work.

When he had cut a dozen logs or so, Ahmek began the harder work of pushing and dragging them towards the ledge. Those that had fallen close to the stream he pushed into the water and let them float with the current till they grounded at the ledge. Soon he had enough logs to start his construction work.

There was no soft mud in the shallow basin below the notch, nothing he could use to anchor the first big log. So Ahmek dived into the stream and found some flat stones that would weigh down one end — the logs were wet with sap so they did not float very high anyway — and began to stack and weave the first network of wood for the base of his dam. Once he had eight or ten good logs in place he brought smaller branches and shoved these into the spaces between the logs. Then twigs into the spaces between the branches. From time to time he instinctively golloped up a few of the leaves from these twigs, but so totally focused was he on his work that he scarcely tasted what he was eating.

Water still rushed and burbled through the gap,

perhaps a little slower now, but so far the network of logs and branches and twigs was more like a sieve than a dam. Ahmek sat up on the ledge and looked at his handiwork and rubbed his paws together, thinking about mud.

"Takin' a break?" the muskrat asked hopefully. He started to sing.

"Now come all you loggers and listen to me," he sang hopefully, in a way that might, he thought, bring an invitation from his new friend to continue.

"What?" Ahmek asked, blinking. "A break? Oh, well, not a long one. I have to get some mud now. D'you know where's there's some good mud? Clay would be nice."

So poor Wah-jusk, starved for company and itching for an audience, resigned himself good-naturedly to the inevitable, supposing that once the work was done, then he might get a chance to show off his singing. He led Ahmek upstream to the nearest meander (where a stream bends and loops back upon itself), and on the inside of the loop there was a small thicket of water plants growing in a mudbank that stretched well back into the grassy flats, towards the granite wall.

Ahmek dived to dig the thick bottom mud with its underneath layer of sticky grey clay. He scooped up a load in his forepaws and swam downstream with the goopy mix of clay and mud till he came — still under-water — to the first of his stone-weighted logs. He plastered the mud around their base, in the spaces between branches and twigs, and went back to the meander for another scoop.

He kept at this task without stopping until the sun was low in the sky. Even when the stars came out he still worked on. On and on, through the night. When light began to creep up in the east again Ahmek was still working.

And then an amazing thing happened. He came to the surface with his latest load of clay and mud. The underwater logs and sticks were watertight now; he had been piling mud on the above-water sticks for the last dozen trips or so. He dumped this latest load into a weave of twigs and grasses and sticks and pebbles, and stepped back to judge his work, when suddenly — like that! — he didn't want to build dam any more. He had had enough.

Now why was that?

There was no more sound of rushing water, that's why. The gap was plugged. The spell was broken. Ahmek could rest.

Whew!

He was really tired. He had been working all the afternoon since he arrived in the meadow, and all the night. A short summer night but all the same. And now it was morning and his work was done for the time being. And he was really tired.

And hungry. There were some sweet grasses at the edge of the stream, and that is what he felt like eating. So he did. The muskrat came and sat beside him.

"That's pretty neat, ya know. You only bin here in my meadow for a day anna night an' lookit what ya done. Never be the same, my old meadow."

Ahmek felt pretty good. "I guess it *is* neat," he said happily, gazing at the interlaced wood and gleaming mud pats that filled the gap, and the water lapping gently a paw's breadth below the top of his little dam.

"Boy," he said contentedly. "Boy!"

"Now listen here," Wah-jusk said. "See, all the other beavers I ever hung around with, they only builden at night and they mostly builden when ya smell winter comin'. This here is only — well, the raspberries is finished but there's still blueberries, so I'd say winter's a while off, hey? Why are you any different?"

Ahmek tried to think about that. "I don't really know," he said. "Maybe you're right, but I just had to build a dam."

He said, "It is only a little one, after all."

Wah-jusk said, "So, who taught ya howda do that?"

Ahmek could not answer that question.

The fact is, nobody had taught him.

Oh, he had helped N'Okomis and N'Osse repair Okwanim — many times. He had helped his mother before the Ningoshkauwin, that terrible day when she disappeared (it seemed distant and clouded, now, that time). But he had never built a dam from nothing and had never seen one built from nothing.

Ahmek could not know how wonderful it is that deep within him, in his blood and his bones, in his genes and his chromosomes, there are precisely written instructions for building a dam. He could not know it any more than you or I could have known, when we were young, that deep inside of us are intricate instructions to make our mouths water when we are hungry and smell food, so that our digestive systems begin to work, or instructions that tell us how to sit up — or *stand up!* — straight, and not fall over, which is a lot harder than you might think. Or most amazing of all, instructions that allow us to watch our spoon fall from the table to the floor when we push it to the edge, and realize, after this has happened a few times, that our mother will always put it back on the table for us and make little cross noises when she does so. And — *and!* — that this will always happen, every time. This particular deeply coded genetic instruction is called "Learning a Law of Nature by Experiment." We humans are the neatest animals of all, in that respect.

But, amazing as we humans are, we do not know how to build dams unless somebody shows us. (Or unless we take the time to think about it and figure it out, which is something that Ahmek would not have been able to do.) It does seem as though we are both pretty amazing, we and the beavers.

Before Ahmek dug himself a small burrow in the soft bank of the stream above the meander, to have a roof over him for his daytime sleep, he had one last set of instinctive instructions to carry out.

He brought another load of mud to the top of the dam. He set it down in a round pat, a sort of mud pie, well up on the rock away from the notch. Then he reached down into the oil sacs between his legs and squeezed out some thick yellow aromatic oil and spread it over the mud pat.

"So they'll know it's yers, right?" Wah-jusk asked.

"That's right," said Ahmek. And off he went to his burrow and lay down flat on his back. Almost immediately Wah-jusk could hear soft snores drifting up from the dark round opening in the bank, as he sat and hummed a romantic little song about the river that fell in love with a swamp, and nobody to hear him at all.

"Oh well," Wah-jusk said to himself. "Maybe later.

TEN   *Kwezenhs*

Ahmek was awakened late in the afternoon by
water lapping at his toes. The burrow had been
dry when he got into it a few hours earlier. Once again
his forepaws twitched because he could hear the sound
of water spilling over the top of his dam. His pond had
begun to fill.

When he came out blinking into the slanting afternoon sunlight his friend the muskrat was nowhere to
be seen, but where there had been nothing but waving
grasses along the banks of the stream, there was now
the shining surface of a little pond. Not much, but it was
a pond, no doubt about that, and with that spillover at
the top of the dam there was a lot of work to be done.

First, though, Ahmek had a careful bath. He
cleaned his nose. He oiled and combed his fur. Then he
carried some mud to dry land at one side of the dam

and spread some aromatic oil on it. The mud pie he had left early in the morning had been washed away by the spillover.

The dam he had built in less than a day was very small, but it was watertight and held back the stream. And so the water level had risen all along the rocky ledge, and now a few poplars were actually standing in shallow water. When Ahmek felled his next tree and cut it into logs, he could easily float his fresh building materials over to the dam. This made the work go much faster.

But it was hard work, all alone, and now that he had spent one day at this dam building, he was a little less captivated by it — only a little. He remembered that all the dam work he had ever done up to now had been with someone else. He remembered that it was easier when one beaver could hold a stick in place while the other packed mud or brought stones to hold it down.

So from time to time, when he paused to catch his breath or sharpen his teeth or nibble on some grass, he found himself thinking of his father and his grandmother and of that fearful dream of his mother, too, in the thunder spirit like a black river, though that thought was, well, really sad.

At dusk, as shadow filled the whole meadow, a voice from a birch tree, just downslope below the dam, said, "Lonely work, ain't it?"

Ahmek peered at the birch, up in its branches, down around its base. He could see nothing. The same voice came floating out of a clump of alders. "Over here, pal."

Ahmek caught on. "Where are you, muskrat?"

Wah-jusk popped up from behind a stone at the end of the dam, nowhere near the birch tree or the alder clump. "Hee, hee, hee!" he cackled. Then he stopped laughing and looked a little sad himself.

"Yeah, well," he said. "All the other beavers I ever seen build a dam had family around. Helpin' out an chattin', away. That got me thinkin about my old . . . . So, where I bin, all day while you was sleepin' and then workin' again here, I bin off traipsin' around the whole territory, downta the big river, up the high rock, see if there's any sign any lady muskrats been by lately. Nope."

He sighed a big sigh. Then he brightened.

"Hey!" Wah-jusk said. "Looka that! You got the spillover stopped again. That's pretty quick work, pal! Wanna take a break now? I can show you where to find some ripe blueberries. Very tasty blueberries."

The two animals swam side by side across the pond towards the place where the stream's gentle flow was swallowed up by the growing broad surface resulting from Ahmek's engineering work. Wah-jusk's long thin tail and Ahmek's wide flat one cut a clean single wake behind them until they arrived at where the water narrowed to the running stream, which had its own ripples that made theirs spread and disappear.

While a faint slash of light from the setting sun was still visible, Wah-jusk led Ahmek up a series of ledges high on the rock wall to a flat place at the top. There they sat together and munched delicious berries, eating companionably, as beavers and muskrat often do, being both very sociable animals. Below them in the meadow they could see the spreading surface of the little pond, where only a day ago there had been nothing but grass and trees. A number of those trees had vanished too.

Wah-jusk said, "Well, that feels better, don't it? Now, you should take it easy for a while, see, before you go back to work."

"What you said about other beavers, building with the family?" Ahmek said. "Well, I am feeling a bit lonely, too." He wiped his nose roughly.

Wah-jusk said kindly, "Aw, come on now. Cheer up, Ahmek. I am gonna sing you a . . . really funny song. It's about, well, listen, you'll hear what it's about."

He stood up on his hind legs on a rock and put his head back and closed his eyes. He cleared his throat, then gave himself a note to start on, "Hummmmmm-mmmmm!" He opened his eyes and said apologetically, "Old voice is a bit rusty, y'know. But here goes."

But before he could begin he suddenly stared over Ahmek's shoulder looking past the beaver towards the dam in the distance. Under his breath he said, "Well I'll be!"

In the dying light of dusk, in the time the French Canadians call "between the dog and the wolf," when Ahmek's new little aquatic creation should have been one unbroken jet-black surface from bank to bank, there was a narrow double streak of reflected light on that surface. It was unmistakably the wake of a swimming animal.

And almost certainly that animal was a beaver.

Wah-jusk and Ahmek watched, frozen with surprise. The sharp forward end of the long arrow of double ripples arrived at the edge of the dam. Ahmek and Wah-jusk both imagined they could see a head at its point. For a moment, Ahmek imagined the head was white.

Whatever it was stopped there, submerged, vanished. Silence. Not a ripple.

Ahmek and Wah-jusk tried to guess where the beaver would surface again, but the intruder had disappeared. They waited in silence for quite a long time. Nothing. Apparently the visitor had been only passing by and had left. Ahmek felt quite deflated and showed it.

"All the same," he said, swallowing nervously and wiping his nose, "I think I had better go and, and see . . . um . . . if . . . um . . . ."

He had entirely forgotten that Wah-jusk had offered to sing to him. He had almost forgotten that Wah-jusk existed. He could think of only one thing. There still just *might* be another beaver in the pond. Maybe, maybe someone he knew, or maybe . . .

Ahmek started cautiously down the path of ledges descending the wall of granite. Wah-jusk watched him go. He hummed tunelessly for a moment. He put on a brave smile, err-hrrmed a couple of times, did a quick buck-and-wing fast step, and recited, "Did'ja ever hear the story of the big fat bat?" No one was listening, of course. "Oh well," Wah-jusk said to himself. "Maybe later."

Ahmek arrived at the edge of his pond and peered over in the deepening darkness towards his dam. No one was there.

He was hoping so much that maybe N'Osse and N'Okomis had caught up with him, or Mudjeekawis, or even a friendly stranger, someone to give him beaver company. Maybe even, he thought, maybe . . . well, don't hope too much.

He was so excited that he could not quite trust his senses. The scent of a strange beaver seemed to waft on a light breeze from the dam. It was not only a stranger, it was . . . well, maybe he could be wrong. Maybe he was imagining it.

His heart was beating fast. He slipped silently into the shallow water and swam forwards with his head up high, to catch every scent.

No moon. It was beginning to get very dark now, the first stars twinkling. Ahmek hardly needed to see. His nose would tell him almost everything. He climbed over the sticks and branches of his new dam, squeezed the water from his fur, and stopped and sniffed in all directions.

There? No. Well, he could not be sure. Perhaps it had all been in his mind. He felt terribly disappointed. He went back into the water and swam slowly around his little pond, among the poplar stumps and the still standing trees, peering and sniffing without success.

Purely out of frustration he started to cut a small tree. He did not need it. He was too upset to be hungry. He just had to have something to do.

Now, when beavers get started on a tree they become very focused on the task. It is even a dangerous time for them, because they are so concentrated, and the noise of their own teeth cutting wood resonates so strongly in their skull bones that they may miss other sounds, signs of danger. If Ahmek had been more alert he might have noticed that he was being watched.

As it was, the first sign that he was certainly not alone came when the small poplar leaned and fell slowly into the pond with a soft swooshing splash. That splash was followed almost immediately by a huge, crack-slap splash from the middle of the pond, a sound that could have been made only by the tail of a beaver.

"I wonder if someone is playing a game?" Ahmek thought. He sank into the water until only his nose and eyes were above the surface. He watched and waited.

There! A slight heave and dip of water not far from the dam, a small dark point emerging, two ripples gleaming, heading for the dam.

And then!

A beaver, a young one almost certainly, a dark-coated beaver, climbed up the bank on its hind legs. This beaver carried a load of mud in its forepaws. It walked slowly along the top of the dam to where Ahmek had laid down his new territorial pat of scented mud, only a few hours before. It paused.

Then it laid down its load of mud and swirled it into a round pat, beside Ahmek's pat, and reached down with its forepaws using the motion beavers always use when they are squeezing out some of their famous scented oil.

When Ahmek blinked it was gone. He headed for the dam. He climbed out and came slowly towards the now very strong scent of . . . the other round pat of mud, beside his own. Fresh wet mud, fresh oil. Ahmek breathed in huge gulps of air. He sat up very still and moved his head around, his nose in the air, sniffing, sniffing. He kept very still.

Silence.

A soft voice came from the water near the far end of the little dam. "I'm over here."

Ahmek slipped into the water. Now he could see a dark head, its nose and ears just above the surface.

The soft voice mewed. It said, "Are you friendly?"

The two beavers swam cautiously towards each other, and then circled an imaginary spot somewhere between them. Then they stopped, noses towards each other, and came closer. A trace of starlight gleamed in one dark eye, and then in another.

Their noses touched.

Ahmek felt a deep warmth flow through his veins and arteries. It was like that feeling when you come almost to the end of an exciting story, and you realize that the dangerous parts are past and everything is going to come out the way it should. Ahmek knew now that this travel, this separation from his family, and this labour to build his own dam and fill his own pond all had a purpose behind it.

Most adolescent beavers leave home at the age of two, to make their own way in the world. If their home pond is a big one, they may remain in it and build a lodge of their own, and find a mate and start a family. But many follow Nature's need for them to strike out, to find new territory, to search for a mate from a different family, a different background, to enrich the beaver race with the mixing of blood and genes and all those mysterious and powerful built-in instructions we call instinct.

Ahmek knew instinctively that he was doing what Nature wanted him to do.

The two beavers stayed nose to nose for a while without moving or speaking.

Then Ahmek said, "You are a girl."

She said, "Yes. My name is Kwezenhs."

"I'm called Ahmek."

They looked at each other in silence, then sank beneath the water together and swam in circles around, over, under. It was a dance of greeting. They came to the surface again and touched and sniffed in the still, silent night. Both of them felt this sense of wonderment, that something had happened which was meant to happen.

But then, all of a sudden, the silence changed. A small sound came from near the top of the dam. A small lapping sound. The two beavers stayed nose to nose, but both of them were listening to the new sound. A moment passed. The lapping sound changed to a rippling sound, and then to a very light gurgling sound. An owl went by overhead, the faint whuff, whuff of its wings. Somewhere up on the rocky ledge, high above them, the thin, cracked voice of a tough old muskrat was crooning an old love song to itself. The gurgling sound took on a chuckle and a faint sloshing, rushing sound. Ever so faint.

Kwezenhs asked, "What now?"

Ahmek said shyly, "Would you like to, ah . . ."

He found it hard to go on.

"Yes?" Kwezenhs said softly.

Ahmek said, "Do you, would you like to, um, come with me and um . . . would you like to help me work on the dam?"

"I would love to!" Kwezenhs said.

And so they did that.

॒॑

With two it goes so much faster. It rained much of the night, but together they worked swiftly and well, and paid no attention to the pelting raindrops. Towards morning they had raised the top of the dam much higher than the water level and left a little dip in the middle where the water could flow through easily without damaging the fabric of the dam when it finally rose to the height they would need to start building a lodge. Ahmek's temporary sleeping burrow was completely flooded now, of course. They dug a small new one as the sun peeped through the eastern trees, and then curled up together, exhausted, and slept very soundly indeed.

The rain clouds blew away towards the middle of the day, while they were still asleep, and then, when the sun was high and hot they came out and had a good swim. They slapped the water with their tails to see who could slap louder. Kwezenhs could. They climbed up on the bank and wrestled and danced for a while. Then they gave each other a Message. There were no words in the Message, but it was a promise and an agreement all at once.

"It was time for me to leave the lodge, that's all," Kwezenhs explained. "Our old pond was too small for more than one family. My brothers went off one way, and I came north, not very far. You and I could go and visit my old gang sometime if you want. But I like it here. I feel like starting something new."

When she talked about visiting the old gang, Ahmek felt a touch of loneliness for N'Okomis and N'Osse, but it passed quickly. He admired Kwezenhs's confidence and her cheerfulness. He was very impressed to find that she could slap the water louder than he could. She was perhaps a little fat for a two-year-old, but he liked that, it seemed comfortable. He especially admired her building skills. She was faster than he was, and very, very sure of herself.

Wah-jusk came to watch them work. Kwezenhs growled a warning, "Stay back!" when the muskrat first came near. But then they became friends, although not very close just yet, as she and Ahmek were intent on their work, while Wah-jusk was more interested in rooting around in his old memory for all the songs he had sung in his youth, hoping his new friends might turn into an audience.

Now Wah-jusk felt even more lonelier than before, watching Ahmek and Kwezenhs together. He doubted that any other muskrat, a lady say, would wander his way. Muskrats are not great travellers. But all the same, he prowled the territory from time to time. Sometimes he disappeared for a whole day or more. When he returned, Ahmek would give him a questioning look, but he would just say, "Nope." And that was that.

The dam was holding very well. The new pond now spread out far into the grove of poplars. It was so big that the volume of water coming into it from the little stream was about the same as the amount that evaporated as sunlight warmed the broad, smooth surface during the day. Now a long time would go by before the level of the pond would rise enough to be noticed.

Ahmek and Kwezenhs found a little hummock towards the northern shore and quickly, with very little mewing or grunting, agreed to start a lodge there. For the next several days they cut logs and sticks and dragged them to the hummock, anchoring them firmly and building them up and up into a rough, round mound.

Ahmek knew that his life was settling into something very solid and sure. He began to get a little careless.

One afternoon as they were plastering mud on the rounded outer shell of their lodge — they had not yet started to dig out the living quarters so it was just a big hill of sticks and mud so far — Ahmek caught a scent that he should have taken as a serious warning, but he was too happy to pay attention.

"Smell that?" Kwezenhs asked him, awhile later, as they took a break to munch on the fat juicy white flesh of a few arrow weed roots she had dug from the bottom of the pond, exactly where the meander had been, its looping mudbanks now three feet underwater.

"I don't like that smell," she said seriously. "What is it, anyway?"

"Oh, it's nothing, I'm sure," Ahmek said. And he sounded very sure. So they went on eating. Then they curled up in the burrow for a little nap before getting back to work.

Bezhen the Lynx, however, was in no doubt whatsoever about what *their* scent meant, and while she was too prudent to risk the danger of their powerful orange teeth by going into the burrow after them, she was a patient hunter. She stayed in the shadows on the north rock face, waiting for the young beavers to come out again.

She did not move until they had finished their baths. Ahmek was putting down a scent pat on the dam, and Kwezenhs was in shallow water cutting poplars.

Ahmek did not hear the stealthy cat approach. He was suddenly overwhelmed by scent. He looked up. The lynx was between him and his one route to safety, the water. The cat smiled a cruel smile and licked her whiskers. Beavers are slow on the ground. Ahmek's eyes darted wildly to one side and the other. There was nowhere he could go. The cat, low to the ground, stared at him. Ahmek stared back. He could not help it. The big oval eyes hypnotized him.

Kwezenhs, watching from the flooded poplar grove, tried to distract the lynx. She growled and screeched. She slapped her tail and dived, and slapped again and dived and came up and screeched. The lynx paid no attention. Hugging the ground, fixing Ahmek with her sharp eyes, she came closer and closer.

"Mudjeekawis," Ahmek thought. "What would you do?"

There was no answer from within or from without.

The cat was two body lengths away. Her haunch and shoulder muscles tensed.

Suddenly a wolf's voice came from behind her, firm, authoritative, cold as snow. "That one's mine, lynx," said the invisible wolf. "Beat it."

"It's mine!" the lynx protested, whipping around wildly, trying to find the wolf in the forest shadows.

The wolf's voice, amazingly, now came from a clump

of cedars on the opposite side of the valley. "Ha, Ha!" the wolf laughed cruelly. "The beaver will be mine, and you will be mine too, cat. Which will I take first? Hmm?"

There was a strange scrabbling sound that was meant to be the sound of a wolf running across the low ground below the dam towards the birches on the other side. The lynx by now was so upset that she took the sound for what it was meant to be, and whirled defensively towards the south. But now another wolf's voice joined the first, from high up on the rock.

"I'm here too, pal," the new wolf said. "You don't like cat meat, pal. Why doncha take the beaver and I'll take that poor quivering lynx, looks scared to death she does."

The lynx, indeed, did look scared to death.

A third wolf's voice came up from the low ground. "Me too, boys. Me too," it said. "We three are about to have a feast. Of beaver and lynx. Delicious, it's gonna be, too. Ready fellas? One, two, three, LET'S GET 'EM!"

Then there was a terrific scrabbling noise that seemed to come from three places at once, although Ahmek would say later, apologetically, that it did sound a bit thin for three seventy-pound wolves on the run, and Wah-jusk would say, yeah, well, he was working on that but after all he was only a two-and-a-half-pound muskrat, and anyway the really serious running sounds were the padded furry feet of the lynx. The cat had had quite enough of her three invisible assailants, and before the light was quite gone from the sky, she was quite gone from the valley, having decided to hunt where voices stayed put and where she could smell wolves before she ever heard or saw them. This ghostly, invisible trio had been quite unlike anything she had ever encountered in her whole entire long and interesting life, or was desirous of encountering ever again.

ELEVEN   *Meanwhile Again*

One day Ahmek said, "My pond at home was called Wiyaunuk. But what should we call this one? We made it, after all. So we should name it. Names are important, don't you think?"

Kwezenhs said, "Sure. Let's call it the Good Water, Onish'shin Nibeesh."

"Be serious," Ahmek said. "That's way too long, 'Onish'shin Nibeesh.' And there are so many "shushing" sounds in it we'll start building dam again every time we say it."

So they called it "Shinibeesh" for short, and that was all right, although it made Wah-jusk laugh. They were all, of course, very good friends now. When Wah-jusk was not off on one of his day trips, looking for a companion, he often ate a meal with them, and as the two beavers hollowed out the interior of the lodge, the muskrat watched them work and chatted away, occasionally offering advice (as an old-time den-digger).

He also began, from time to time, to sing them a few of the old songs from his younger days. Soon, he was sure, they would be ready to take some time off and he could put on a real concert and truly amaze them.

᛭

Some distance down from Kwezenhs and Ahmek's dam, the stream wound its way through a sunny, relatively open cedar bush and eventually reached the big river, the river humans call the Oxtongue.

Returning up the Oxtongue towards Canoe Lake, the three painters, Jim MacDonald, Alex Jackson, and Lawren Harris, stopped for lunch in the quiet little backwater where the stream reached the river.

"Look at that, Jim," Alex Jackson said. "When we had lunch here on the way down, a week ago, that stream was running quite fast. I think there was even a little white water right here where it falls into the river. Now it's just a trickle. We've had a day and a night of rain, so it's not drought. What do you suppose . . .?"

"Beavers, I should say," said Jim, who had already started a small sketch of an old campsite with a big poplar in it, right across the river from where they had stopped. "I bet they're making a new dam upstream, maybe not too far."

Lawren Harris looked up from the little pad he was always sketching in and said, "Hey, Jim. Why don't you scout it out, and if you're right we could take the camera up there and see what we can get?"

Jim was back in an hour. "Beaver all right," he said. And so the three friends took their heavy black camera with its big bellows and stout wooden tripod and made their way up the brook until they came to a very new beaver dam built along a natural rocky ledge, at the end of a valley formed by high rock walls. The midday sun beat down upon a wide spread of water in which there grew hundreds of young poplars, still green and lively. Not far from the dam a very large number of stumps were newly cut. This was clearly a very new pond. The branches forming the dome of the lodge over towards the north shore were newly cut too; many of them were still in leaf.

The men made themselves a blind with some balsam boughs, set up the camera, and stayed very still for about an hour. They were rewarded by the arrival of two handsome young beavers, who suddenly surfaced and swam to the dam to make mud pies, and ate some grass very close to the camera blind. But when Lawren snapped the camera shutter, one of the beavers sat up very straight, listening and sniffing. Then suddenly the two of them slid into the water, both slapping their tails very loud (but one louder than the other), and disappeared again.

"Never mind!" Lawren said. "I've got a great shot."

They headed back to their lunch spot and there they found four men in two black canoes, pulled up by the shore, looking suspiciously at the red canoe and the painting gear. They turned menacingly at the sound of the artists approaching, but when they saw that there were three of them, they softened their stance.

One of the men addressed the tallest and most impressive member of the group. "Any sign of beavers up there?"

"You fellas trapping beaver?" Lawren asked, gravely. "I thought that was against the law in this park."

The man made a fist and raised it — but one of the others, sensing that they had better be careful with these three painters, put a hand on the first man's arm and said, almost politely, "Well, sir, you're right. It is against the law. But, you see, times is really hard. We all been outta work for months now, me and these other fellas here. Got wounded overseas in the war, shipped home again, sposed to be good veteran's benefits and all, but didn't last long and now we're down on our luck. We don't like to break the law. But we talked it over with the Park Ranger and he said, 'Look fellas, I'll turn a blind eye fer a few days long as you don't say nothin' about it to nobody. Park's overstocked with beaver right now.' Well it don't look overstocked to us.

"Anyway, it's fer science, see? Guys in a lab in Toronto. They need live animals to test for some medicine. They give 'em this horrible disease and then try to cure 'em with this . . . wonder drug, they call it. Then they cut 'em up when they're still alive to see how the drug's workin, see. Beaver, otter, mink, muskrat. Live. Something about water animals. Secret stuff but we can tell you, I reckon. Beaver's what they specially want. Don't ask why."

Jim MacDonald whispered in Lawren's ear, "They don't look much like ex-soldiers to me. I bet these are the guys Tom told us about." The painters had noticed a couple of boxes with airholes and peg locks in the dirty black canoes.

The man continued, "Well, we ain't had very good luck. So we'd really like to know if you seen any beavers up there."

Jim MacDonald, painter and a vice-president of the distinguished Toronto printing and lithograph company, Grip Limited, and a truthful man, looked at the faces of these four men in the black canoes, one by one, for a moment. And then he shook his head and said, "No. No beavers up there. Not a sign."

The four men stared hard at the painters, for a minute looking as though they didn't believe them. Then one of them turned abruptly and said, "Well, thanks anyway," and all four got back into the canoes and paddled away.

TWELVE   *Wind from the North*

The birch leaves turned to yellow; the maples red-
dened and their leaves began to drift lazily down
whenever a breeze passed by. Some mornings there
were dancing points of light all up the grasslands east
of the pond, as the sun climbed through mist. The mist
lay thick where the water was still warmer than the
night-cooled rocks and trees. One morning, hoarfrost
made a glistening coat on leaves and twigs and spears
of grass; it stayed there till the sun was high enough to
melt it off.

That first frost was a signal to Ahmek and
Kwezenhs to start cutting food for the winter. Now the
face of the forest changed, bare branches and twigs,
dark green in the pines and spruce and cedar. Only the
oaks and the beeches still held their leaves, the oak a
dark copper, the beeches sand-coloured. The two young

beavers worked night and day cutting young poplars all across the pond and the meadow beyond.

For weeks they dragged big branches down to the bottom of the pond, embedding the thick ends in the mud, and then lacing smaller ones among them. They were building a kind of underwater forest, close to the plunge hole entrances to the lodge. Their instincts had told them how. They were not *planning* for the winter; they were carrying out deep and mysterious instructions from within.

If you had the power to fly, if you could hover over Shinibeesh like a giant dragonfly and then beat your wings harder and harder so that you rose higher and higher and soon could see other ponds and streams and lakes, spreading out below you . . . and if you had eyesight as powerful as a great space telescope, so that you could see all the other beavers in all the other ponds, thousands and thousands of them, you would see that they were all doing the same thing. And not one of them really knew *why* they were doing it; only that they must.

One morning, as they swam to the dam to inspect it, Ahmek and Kwezenhs found needles of ice, glassy spears lancing out onto the surface of Shinibeesh from the rocks at the south end of the dam, where it was shaded throughout most of the day from the warming rays of the sun. Every day the sun was lower in the sky.

Cattail roots were rich and tasty now. Kwezenhs and Ahmek sat on the dam and munched and munched, storing up vitamins and getting fat for the winter. One afternoon they looked up together from their feast of roots, and Wah-jusk was sitting there on a rock near the end of the dam, watching them silently with an odd look on his mischievous old face. They had not heard him coming.

"Guess what," Wah-jusk said with a sly smile. "See, I decided to go all the way down to the big river, fer a look-see. Never went down that far before, maybe when I was a kid with my old man. Well, whaddya know, I see some traces, see? One o' my kind's been by. And, uh, well . . ."

Kwezenhs said, "Well? Well, Wah-jusk? Are you going to tell us or not?" (But she knew, of course.)

"Well, uh," Wah-jusk hesitated. Then he turned and called out in his creaky old voice, "Hey, honey, come out now and meet the beavers. Don't be shy."

A plump, dark-furred muskrat came forward timidly from the clump of grasses where she had been hiding.

Wah-tessanaugh was a bit shy. She was also much younger than Wah-jusk. Kwezenhs decided to call her Tess for short. That seemed to make her feel a little less shy. Ahmek gave her a tasty cattail root and encouraged her to eat with them. After a while she wiped her whiskers daintily with both forepaws and told her story.

"I had a terrible experience," she said. "I was living alone a long way from here. I think it was a long way. I am not very clear about where I am now. Because two days ago when I came out of my den in the morning there was a strange smell, and suddenly something made a loud noise, bang! And I was caught by the tail. Look."

She turned around, a bit shy still, and showed where part of her tail was missing, and a wound there, still very sore.

"And some Humans came and took me. I was sure they were going to kill me. They put me in a box. They put the box in a sort of log that they floated along in. They made strange talking noises, but I could not understand. But one of the Humans seemed to like me. He took me out of the box to feed me. He tried playing with me. The others made cross noises at him, but he seemed to like playing with me, and I bided my time.

"He took me out to play and feed after dark and I just slipped through his hands and ran. He couldn't see me in the dark. I ran for the river bank and swam as hard as I could. To get away from those strange black logs the Humans floated in, so fast they were. But they couldn't see me.

"And then, oh dear, I had no idea where I was or where to go, and I met this kind gentleman here. And, you know? He sang me the nicest song."

Here her nose and ears turned a bit red and she lowered her eyes and looked at the ground.

"And we have decided to . . ."

She could not go on.

"Well, that's just lovely," Kwezenhs said.

Snow had begun to fall.

"Come on, honey," Wah-jusk said. "Come and see the family homestead. Gotta bit more work to do, put in some more food, stuff like that. We'll see you beavers later."

And off they went.

"That's good," Ahmek said. "Now we don't have to worry about him for the winter."

He was wrong about that, as it would turn out.

On the third day after the arrival of Tess, large ice
patches spread out into the pond from the south and
west shores. Great long howling gusts of wind swept
down into their valley from the north, carrying a fine,
hard snow. A cutting cold, that wind, if you were out in
it. For the beavers it was actually warmer to be in the
near-frozen water.

The narrow channel between the lodge and the
shore behind it was frozen: solid. Late one afternoon
Ahmek climbed up the bank at the north end of the
dam where the sun struck it most of the day. No ice had
formed there yet. Ahmek walked through the light
snow all around the pond. He stepped out onto the ice
behind the lodge. He felt uneasy on the ice. He didn't
like the snow much, either. He felt better as soon as he
came to a smooth mudbank sloping to the water. The
water was very cold, but his winter growth of fur, well
oiled every morning, kept him dry and warm. He had a
good layer of fat on him, too; that helped.

The sun had gone below the trees by the time he
started swimming back towards the lodge. There was
no breeze. All the colours were gone. The treetrunks
were black against the snow.

Silence.

Ahmek stopped swimming to listen to the silence.

Every few moments there would be a tinkling
sound, as new ice crystals suddenly formed where an
instant before there had been black water. Just a crack-
ling tinkle. Then nothing.

A voice from the direction of the dam said quietly,

"The rest is silence."

There was a white shape on the dam. A tall white beaver stood there, almost invisible against the snow.

"Mudjeekawis! Mudjeekawis!" Ahmek called out happily.

As he came up the plunge hole into the lodge, Ahmek said to Kwezenhs, where she sat combing her fur, "We have a visitor."

Mudjeekawis climbed up on the ledge and gravely squeezed the water from his fur, before doing anything else. Then he bowed very low, very dignified, to Kwezenhs. "Madam," he said courteously and looked at her, squinting. "She walks in beauty like the night," he said to Ahmek.

Kwezenhs giggled. "Well, for heaven's sake!" she said, but not rudely. Ahmek had told Kwezenhs about the odd way that Mudjeekawis sometimes spoke. So she was not really surprised. She thought it was cute, the way he talked.

Mudjeekawis cleared his throat. He said, "In the time of the Silence there must be some wisdom. That is my task in life."

He said, "As I have undertaken to share with you some of my little store of knowledge and wisdom, I thought it apt to visit your winter store of provisions . . ."

"That means 'food,'" Ahmek whispered to Kwezenhs.

"Shh!" she said. "Don't interrupt him. Besides, I know what it means!"

Mudjeekawis did not seem to notice this exchange. ". . . to visit your winter store of provisions," he repeated, "and satisfy myself that you go well to the hivernal season."

The two young beavers were not quite sure what this meant. They had done what their instincts had told them to do and stopped doing it when their instincts told them it was enough. Why anyone would want to examine what they had done was not clear, but Mudjeekawis spoke with great authority; so they understood that this was important.

The three of them went into the water. Ahmek led the way. By now he was able to shoot out of the submarine entrance with even more force than old N'Okomis used to have.

"I'm a regular torpedo," he thought. "I hope Mudjeekawis noticed."

Mudjeekawis circled their tangled underwater mass of twigs and branches and leaves. It was far bigger than the lodge itself. Here and there the big white beaver stopped to nibble a twig or a leaf. Then he rolled his eyes upwards, considered, then nodded approval.

They returned to the lodge and squeezed the water from their fur before going up to the upper level.

Presently, Mudjeekawis said, "You do understand, I hope, that to every thing there is a season; a time to plant, and a time to pluck up that which is planted. Well, now, that is a very fine food store you have made. Very fine. More than enough. You will be well fed all through the winter."

The young beavers tried to understand these words. They dimly knew that soon the pond would be closed. Ice was taking over more of the surface every day. They did understand that they would eat the underwater food supply. But they had no idea that there might *not* be food some day, nor that the winter could be a menace to them.

It is difficult for us humans to understand that beavers cannot really think ahead. Mudjeekawis was somehow different in this respect.

Kwezenhs showed Mudjeekawis a pile of fresh, crisp cattail roots she had brought in for supper.

"Will you stay and have supper with us?" she said. "These are really good and really fresh."

"Oh no, I, well, I probably should be going now, you know, continue my, ahh . . ."

They waited, but he did not finish his sentence.

Ahmek said, "Are you looking after some other beavers? Keeping an eye on them the way you seem to be doing for us?"

"Ah, well now, not really, I just, um, ought to be getting along, and, uh . . . ." Mudjeekawis's eyes kept wandering towards the cattail roots. He licked his lips.

Kwezenhs asked him a second time; she had been well brought up. She said politely, "Well, of course, if you must. But you shouldn't miss these lovely cattail roots, they're almost all gone now, you know? And these ones are especially nice."

"Ah, well, that's very kind, I'm sure," Mudjeekawis said politely. "But I have to be . . . ah . . . getting, ah . . . ."

He looked over the edge of the upper level down towards the plunge hole and its dark cold water. He rocked a couple of times as though he were about to move. But Ahmek could see that his mouth was watering a little.

Ahmek said quietly, "Kwezenhs might feel that you thought her cattails are not as fine as what a Great White Beaver is used to. Please stay and have a few with us."

"Oh dear, of course I would not want her to think that!" Mudjeekawis whispered quickly. Then he said to Kwezenhs, "Well, of course, you are right, it would be a shame to miss these lovely roots."

They all sat around munching and murmuring little satisfied mewing noises. Mudjeekawis talked to himself. All beavers talk to themselves, but the tall white old fellow talked even more than N'Okomis used to. N'Okomis had been easier to understand, too.

Mudjeekawis said, or hummed, something that sounded like, "Go and catch a falling star." (Hum, hum, munch, schlurp.) "Get with child a mandrake root." (Hum, hum.) "Tell me what I dreamt last night." (Hum, hum . . . munch, munch, schlurp, schlurp.)

But Ahmek whispered to Kwezenhs, "All the same, I'm glad I was able to make him change his mind and stay for supper."

Kwezenhs looked at him sharply. "You didn't make him change his mind. He was waiting to be asked three times. Didn't your mother ever teach you that?"

"No, I never knew that," Ahmek said. And Kwezenhs was immediately sorry, because she knew the sad story of the Ningoshkauwin, the terrible time when Ahmek's mother had disappeared.

Occasionally Mudjeekawis burped a small burp. But very polite, behind his paw.

As they were grooming themselves after their meal, Ahmek said, "Where is your lodge, Mudjeekawis? Where will you be when the ice is everywhere? Is it close by here?"

Mudjeekawis sat up straight and whipped his

broad white tail around and sat on it. He leaned sideways until it seemed as though he must fall over. He spoke more to the dome at the top of the lodge than to the young beavers.

He said, "Actually, I was thinking of going south for the winter. I have heard that this is a very good thing to do. I was talking to some Waewaes, you know, the great geese. They were on their way south, they said. They said, they said . . . it is not wise to stay here when the ponds freeze over. So I thought . . ."

Kwezenhs whispered, "I think he hopes we'll ask him to stay."

"To stay!" Ahmek whispered back. "With us? He would never. He's a . . . ." Ahmek stopped and looked at her. "Are you serious?"

She nodded, yes.

"Okay," thought Ahmek, doubtfully. He said aloud to Mudjeekawis, a little bit shyly, "Look, ah, why don't you stay with us for the winter?"

Mudjeekawis nearly fell over sideways. He recovered his balance and said quickly, "Oh no, I couldn't do that, I think really I should be going along, you have a nice little home here, I wouldn't want to . . . ummm."

Ahmek whispered to Kwezenhs, "You see; he doesn't *want* to stay!"

Kwezenhs shook her head. "Three times!" she whispered.

"Oh!" Ahmek thought. So he said, "Would you like any more cattail roots?"

"Well, they were very good, but I've had enough," Mudjeekawis said.

Ahmek said, "Well, I wish you would consider staying here. We have lots of room. And you said yourself we have lots of food."

Mudjeekawis smiled. He knew it was going to be all right now. He said, "Well you are very kind. Of course I knew you would be kind. But really, I couldn't."

Ahmek nodded to Kwezenhs. He was beginning to enjoy this new game. He said, "Listen, please, it would be great, we would have a great time together, we. . . ." But Kwezenhs broke in. It was her turn now.

She said, mischievously, "Now, Ahmek, Mudjeekawis knows best. He is a Wise One, after all. We mustn't stand in his way." And she smiled at Mudjeekawis, a big orange toothy beaver kind of a smile, and nodded towards the plunge hole.

Mudjeekawis's confidence was a bit shaken. Kwezenhs seemed serious. He had been brought up in a family like Kwezenhs's family, he was sure, and she should know the rules, and he had only been asked twice.

Ahmek was totally puzzled at what was going on.

Mudjeekawis waddled down to the edge of the plunge hole, turned around, and said, "Well good-bye, ah, children, I hope you —"

"Dear Mudjeekawis," Kwezenhs interrupted, "I was thinking. Those Waewaes? About going south? They don't . . . *walk* south, do they?"

Mudjeekawis looked back over his shoulder, hopefully. "I don't suppose they do," he said.

Kwezenhs said, "Well, no. They fly, don't they? I think that means it is very far, this south they go to, hmm?"

There was a pause. Mudjeekawis seemed to be

getting his confidence back. "Well," he said, "I suppose you are right about that."

"Yes," she said, "I believe I am. But you can't fly, even if you are very magical and very wise. And perhaps it is a bit far to walk. So really, dear Mudjeekawis, I really think you should accept our offer and stay here with us in our nice new lodge."

Mudjeekawis chuckled then. "Ahmek," he said happily, "your Kwezenhs is a very wise lady, wouldn't you agree?"

THIRTEEN   *The World Beneath the Ice*

On most days when the sun shone brightly the three beavers took a trip around the pond, under the ice. Kwezenhs particularly rejoiced in these trips and would often strike off ahead of the others, disappearing in the dark waters far ahead of them and charging back after a few minutes with a look in her eyes that seemed to say, "Come on, you slowpokes!"

A beaver can stay underwater almost fifteen minutes without breathing, but a trip around the pond took longer than that. So they would watch for bubbles under the ice, little domes where pockets of air were trapped, and stick their noses up into those pockets of ice-capped air to get a fresh breath before swimming on.

One day Kwezenhs was already breathing at an unusually large air dome when Ahmek and Mudjeekawis caught up with her. With almost all of her head out of the water she could talk, and she called down to them, "Watch this!"

Kwezenhs sank down into the water away from the air dome. Under the ice there was a world all of its own, topped with a white ceiling, darker in places where the snow had drifted above, sometimes smooth, sometimes cracked, sometimes decorated with rolls and knobs as well as air holes. The light was pearly and magical. And everywhere was the icy ceiling, like an upside-down skating rink only rougher. It looked perfectly round because the visibility under it was the same in all directions, so everywhere you looked, the farthest place you could see was the same distance away.

Kwezenhs rolled over on her back under this circular roof. She floated up till her tummy was against the upside-down ice rink. Then she stuck her feet up above her and began to walk, upside down, on the ceiling of ice.

Ahmek forgot he was underwater and started to laugh and almost choked. Mudjeekawis was nodding back and forth as if he were about to break into bubbles of laughter. The two of them rolled on their backs, too, and floated up to the ice and began to walk upside down on the ceiling just like Kwezenhs. Mudjeekawis's white fur was so like the ceiling above them that he looked like a mound of ice walking.

Presently Kwezenhs made a sign that indicated, "Now watch *this!*" She stopped walking and swung her head down so that her tail and hind feet were up there against the roof of ice. Moving her tail beneath her — well, really *above* her — she looked just as if she were sitting there chatting away in the upper room, only she was really on the ceiling upside down.

Immediately Ahmek and Mudjeekawis had to do the same. They all began to rock back and forth, needing to laugh. In a moment they were practically bursting with laughter, and they had to swim quickly to Kwezenhs's big air dome and stick their heads into the air pocket and cackle and hoot for a while.

Mudjeekawis showed them another trick. Sometimes when they felt close to running out of breath, there were no air domes in sight. But there were always domes or hollows of some kind in the ice — places where the ice had heaved up or perhaps once had air in them but now were filled with water. Even though the water was right up to the top of them, Mudjeekawis showed them a way to use them to breathe. He came up just beneath one such hump in the ice and breathed out a gush of bubbles, all the air in his lungs. The bubbles rose into the water-filled dome. The dome trapped the bubbles and soon became a small air dome, with breathed-out air in it.

Mudjeekawis then waited for a minute or so with empty lungs, letting the stale part of his breath sink to the bottom of this bubble of trapped used air, then he could breathe most of it in again.

This was not as sweet as fresh air, but it was enough to get them to the next natural air dome. As the days got colder and the ice got thicker, the bottom of the ice became rougher and rougher, so that there were lots of domes they could breathe from, or re-breathe.

On one trip they found a good supply of cattail roots in the mud, not yet frozen, in a part of the pond they had not foraged before. This day was very cold, punishingly cold. While they were digging the roots they could hear creaking and snapping as new ice formed above them. They would dig a few roots, find air domes to breathe in, munch a root or two, and dig some more. It took some time to gather a supply to take back to the lodge.

Then, because they were carrying as many roots as possible in their forepaws, it took them longer than usual to swim back to the lodge. They were tired, too, so they took extra time resting at air domes.

If you had been visiting the pond that day you would not have known that three strong beavers were cruising under the ice. There was no sign of their movement.

There was a sign, though, that the lodge was empty.

When beavers are in their lodge in winter, there is always a faint wisp of mist or "steam" rising from the small vent at the top. The lodge is kept warm by the body heat of its inhabitants. This warmth keeps the water at the top of the plunge holes from freezing. If you had been at the pond that day, you might have noticed that there was no mist rising from the vent in the lodge. You might have wondered if it was getting pretty cold in there.

It was.

When the three beavers returned to the lodge, Kwezenhs was the first to go up. In a second she came backing out of the tunnel, looking scared. Ahmek went up to look. They had been away too long. The lodge had gotten very cold. The surface of the water at the top of the plunge hole had frozen over hard. They could not get in, to air and safety. They needed to breathe, badly.

Ahmek came back down and stared questioningly at Mudjeekawis. *What to do?* Mudjeekawis put his head close to Ahmek's and sent the strong young beaver a Message.

Ahmek swam quickly to the other side of the lodge and disappeared into the back entrance. Kwezenhs and Mudjeekawis could hear him scrabbling and pushing up in there, using every bit of his strength to bang his dark head against the ice cap.

Mudjeekawis's eyes were beginning to get red from holding his breath so long. His chest hurt. Kwezenhs looked frightened.

There was a cracking sound from above. The water flowed and receded by them where they waited by the back entrance. They raced up the tunnel to find a ring of broken ice at the top where Ahmek had finally bumped and chewed and banged and wiggled and forced his way through. They gasped, filling their lungs.

Mudjeekawis lay on his back on the lower level, panting like a puppy. He did not even take the time to squeeze the water from his fur. His eyes were closed. He just waved a paw at the two younger beavers and lay there for several minutes more until his breath slowed down.

"The ice was here, the ice was there," he panted. "The ice was all around."

"It sure was," Ahmek said.

"It cracked and growled and roared and howled," Mudjeekawis said, "like noises in a swound."

Ahmek and Kwezenhs shrugged, puzzled. What did that mean? They had heard a few cracks. But howls? And what was a "swound?"

Well, there was no time for that. Ahmek jumped and stamped on the ice at the top of the front plunge hole. After a few jumps he had cracked it, too. Then he could get a paw in, and then his teeth, and in a few minutes he had it clear. Then he finished clearing away all the remaining collar of ice where he had broken through the back entrance.

He swam up and down both tunnels several times, to make sure they were clear. He brought up the cattail roots they had dropped on the bottom. Nobody was hungry. They were all very tired though.

One by one they dropped off to sleep. From time to time Ahmek awoke, checked the two plunge holes, and cleaned away any thin ice that formed during those first few hours. By then their body heat had warmed the place, and the plunge holes were safe again as long as someone dived in them from time to time to keep the water moving.

"That was a close one," Ahmek said. "Boy!"

Mudjeekawis said, as they had a meal of cattail roots, "One winter when I was a boy." Then he stopped. They waited.

He continued, "Well, I am not sure whether I am remembering this, or whether it is a dream I had just now. But I think it is a memory. Thanks for the memory. Hmm, hmm, hmm, hmm . . ." He hummed a little melody. They waited.

"Oh yes," Mudjeekawis said. "Yes, we were trapped inside the lodge for many days. We got very hungry. We started to eat the branches and twigs in the roof and sides of the lodge. The branches it was built with. It was very old, dry wood. But it was all we had. By the time things warmed up enough to melt the ice, we had eaten away so much of the dome that when the mud thawed out, the lodge fell in on us. Yes, it's a memory, it's very clear now."

Ahmek sat up suddenly and said, "Wah-jusk!"

"What about Wah-jusk?"

"We haven't seen him for several days, since the beginning of this cold spell! He and Tess usually visit every couple of days!"

"Well, look," Mudjeekawis said. "We must not leave the lodge empty. Go you forth and see what you can see, and come and report. And your lady and I shall keep the lodge warm and keep the plunge holes free."

"I will," Ahmek said.

It was a good thing he did. The tiny entrance to Wah-jusk's den was plugged with ice. Ahmek could hear faint scratching and the sound of a tired, small voice calling out from above. He could not make out what the voice said, but he could guess.

There was still some wet mud at the very bottom of Wah-jusk's entrance tunnel. Ahmek began to dig and tear at the roots around it with his teeth and claws. There was a small air dome close by. He put his nose into it to breathe, and then called out. "I'm coming, Wah-jusk. I'm coming, Tess!" He couldn't tell if they heard him. Would he be in time?

It was tiring work. He needed to breathe pretty often. The air dome was too small. For his next breath he swam the hundred feet back to the lodge and instructed Mudjeekawis and Kwezenhs as to how they must help. All the rest of the day they took turns, the three beavers, one or two digging and clawing upward, chipping away at the plug of ice while at least one of them stayed in the lodge to keep it warm.

It was getting dark before Ahmek and Kwezenhs together broke through into the little den above. The air was very stale. Every bit of stored root and grass and leaf had been eaten. The place was a mess. The two muskrats were unconscious or asleep. They were desperately thin and their fur was dull and matted.

Kwezenhs and Ahmek rubbed them and shook them and warmed them till they woke up. "Can you hold your breath for two minutes?" Ahmek said. The muskrats nodded, scared, yes, they thought they could. The beavers half dragged, half pushed, helping them swim to the lodge.

Once inside, the beavers gave them a good feed. After a bit Wah-jusk paused in his eating, with a clutch of wet grasses hanging out of his mouth. He looked gratefully at Ahmek. "Thanks, pal," he croaked, with his mouth full.

Ahmek thought about a certain lynx on the dam one day, not so long ago. "I owed you one," he said to Wah-jusk.

The two brave, bedraggled little rodents finished their meal and went back to sleep. They stayed with the beavers for almost a week, getting their strength back, before heading home to repair their own den.

🐾

The days got shorter and shorter. The beavers slept a great deal. But every day there was a visit to the muskrats or a visit from them, to make sure.

Then, one day, they felt that the days were getting just a little longer again. In the afternoons they sometimes went for long swims under the pearly ice. The ice was darker now and very thick. Thicker than the length of a beaver from muzzle to tail tip.

It was the time that humans call February.

Both Kwezenhs and Ahmek felt strange forces moving in their blood. They were restless, but they spent hours huddled close together, as if to keep warm, although in the snug little lodge they were quite warm enough. They had lots to eat, and their bodies were still plump and healthy.

One morning, when they woke, they found Mudjeekawis standing tall, on the lower level, his tail under him, his eyes closed.

This felt important, somehow. The two young beavers came and sat at the feet of the tall, mysterious, eccentric old fellow.

After a while he opened his eyes and looked at them kindly.

"I have told you that for everything there is a season," he said. "And a time under Kitchi Manitou for every purpose." He looked at them fondly. "A time to be born and a time to die," he said. For a terrible moment Ahmek feared that Mudjeekawis was going to tell them some bad news. But no.

Mudjeekawis now began to look a little embarrassed. His pink nose turned pinker. "Ahh herrrm," he said. ". . . Ah ummm. There is also . . . ahh herrrm . . . well, children, there is a time to love, too. That is what you have been . . . feeling these last few days. Come."

It was time for a Message. The three of them stood

together, their forepaws clasped around each other,
their heads touching. They swayed back and forth. A
great Message passed between Mudjeekawis and the
two young beavers, but it was a secret so we shall
respect that. It was about the deepest, most profound
force in life.

They swayed back and forth, mewing softly in their
throats.

Then Mudjeekawis sighed. "Ah, well," he said softly.
He hugged them again, waddled up into the upper
chamber, and curled up in his sleeping place.

Ahmek and Kwezenhs stood with their heads
together for a moment and made each other a Message.
Then, without speaking, they slipped down into the
plunge hole, and deep, deep, in the dark water of
Shinibeesh, under the pearl-coloured, world-round roof
of ice. Ahmek swam on his back, Kwezenhs swam
above him. Their eyes were closed and they were
perfectly together.

Rise up again now, up, up into the winter sky over
Shinibeesh as you did once before. Hover as if you were
a magical winter dragonfly. Look widely, at all those
circles of ice, those frozen ponds, the snow-covered
beaver dams, the world-round roofs of ice spreading
wide, wide, to the edges of the known world beneath
your magical vision. In all those frozen ponds, under
all those roofs of ice, young beavers are swimming
together, silent, yet saying all there is to say.

New life is forming.

FOURTEEN   *Spring*

The winter food store held out well, but eating it was just a necessity, no longer a pleasure. The cut ends of the twigs and branches had gone brown, and the taste — even of the youngest, tenderest bark — was stale. The three beavers slept more than ever, although the light through the ice cap was getting stronger and stronger day by day, and its rich blue colour was becoming more pearly, a touch of yellow in it here and there. When they took their survey trips around the pond, they found more air domes to breathe in every day, and they found themselves glancing eagerly in all directions, imagining a touch of sky.

Kwezenhs slept more than the others did. Beavers are great talkers, but these days Kwezenhs did not say much. She smiled secretly to herself and seemed very pleased.

While Ahmek and Mudjeekawis followed their instincts and ate less, letting their layers of fat help nourish them now as the air filtering through the vent at the top of the lodge grew balmier and more fragrant, Kwezenhs ate greedily and got rounder day by day.

Wah-jusk stuck his head in the door one day and said, "Guess what, folks! There's gonna be a few more muskrat voices in the pond pretty soon, whaddya know about that!"

Kwezenhs smiled her secret smile.

And then there came that wonderful night when Ahmek woke up to hear Mudjeekawis returning from a swim, and smelled something he hadn't smelled all winter. He could hardly believe it. He looked over the edge of the sleeping level. In the pale moonlight filtering through the vent he could see what looked like a dark mass lying on the lower level as the big white beaver solemnly squeezed the water from his fur.

"Where have you been?" Ahmek asked.

Mudjeekawis chuckled mischievously. "Going to and fro upon the Earth," he said. "And walking up and down upon it." Ahmek did not get it. But he suddenly realized what the dark green mass was.

Cedar branches, green, glistening, fresh cut — the rich aroma filled the lodge.

Beavers do not usually enjoy the taste of evergreen leaves and twigs; there is a strong, bitter, turpentine quality that is like old-fashioned human medicines that were supposed to be good for you. Indeed, these leaves *are* good for the beavers, lots of vitamins. But they make the lips pucker.

Still, they smelled of the outdoors; before he could

help himself Ahmek was nibbling at their tangy, bitter leaves, and it felt good, it felt lively.

Kwezenhs slipped quietly down beside him and sniffed and began to nibble, too.

Mudjeekawis watched them as if he had a secret to tell. His eyes were dancing.

Kwezenhs caught it. "Well?" she asked.

"How soft the moonlight sleeps on yonder bank," the white beaver said. "By the dam. There is even a small trickle going over. Come. See!"

The water was black as black, but the ice above was white as white. As they approached the dam they could hear the faintest gurgling of running water and their paws began to twitch for building.

They came up, right beneath the overflow, and there was open water, and they were out again, into the air, after four months under the ice. The air smelled of old leaves and new leaves, mud, the forest. Smells that for days had teased them in the tiniest quantities through the breathing hole were now all around them.

The world had turned upside down again; the ice was now beneath, instead of above, them. They stayed outdoors all night till the moon went down and the sky began to pale. They cut down, in the space of a few hours, twenty-six young poplar trees plus, by mistake, one maple in which they were not really interested at all. And one hasty bite out of a spruce tree made Kwezenhs's lips curl and stung her tongue.

They were serenely wasteful; they stripped off only the smallest twigs, the thinnest, tenderest bark. They left a scandalous amount of perfectly good food

untouched. They rolled and mewed and laughed and
rocked. They occasionally burped loud burps.

Only a few days later there was a long lead of open
water where the stream flowed into the east end of
Shinibeesh. Three or four young speckled trout were
fanning their tails in the sunlight where the brook
bubbled and swirled out of its narrow banks. The fishes
looked up calmly with their round eyes as Ahmek and
Kwezenhs came up from under the ice for a scent of the
fresh flowing water. Three days after that, the same
open water reached almost halfway to the top of the
lodge, which was still surrounded by ice, but with a
band of dark water where the warmth of the lodge itself
had melted a kind of ring all around its perimeter.

Ahmek and Kwezenhs climbed up the snowy bank
on the south side, which was still in shadow most of the
day, and sat on their tails and slid down the snow like
tobogganers till they bumped on the ice at the edge of
the pond. The ice broke under them and they plopped
through into the water, came up laughing, climbed the
snowy bank, and did it again just for fun.

On the north shore, which was now in sunlight
most of the day, the snow was nearly all gone, and
green shoots were pushing up through the fragrant
earth. Once, as Ahmek was nibbling at the sweet, short
grasses, he saw a movement, and a tiny brown lizard
with orange spots oozed its slim shape out of the mud
and blinked in the sunlight.

Two evenings later, they came out of the lodge to
find a streak of open water stretching from the lodge up
to the inlet where they had seen the trout. And they
heard a new spring sound: thousands and thousands of

small piping voices coming from tiny green frogs who climb into the trees and sing about love all night long. These are the loudest sounds, per gram weight of animal producing them, in all of the animal kingdom.

Soon there was no ice at all left in the pond, except in some of the shaded inlets on the south side. Kwezenhs called Ahmek to her as she sat near a receding snowbank on this shaded side. As he came close she stood up and held out her forepaws. He did the same. They clung together for a long Message. It was deep and mysterious and joyful all at once, and there were new voices in it, voices that had never been in the world before.

And now it was May. Mudjeekawis came up on the shore beside them as they were about to head back to the lodge at dawn. The three of them watched the sunlight begin to edge down to the pond through the trees at the east end of Shinibeesh. Flecks of green were in the branches of the poplars, and the purple colour in the still naked birches was like grapes. A kingfisher swooped low. Two ducks, American goldeneyes, drifted silently by the north shore. A bullfrog croaked.

Mudjeekawis said happily, "More matter for a May morning."

"What?" asked Kwezenhs.

"All in the merry month of May," sang Mudjeekawis. "When green buds they were swellin'." And he plunged into the water still burbling away and headed for the lodge.

FIFTEEN

One and Two

One day Kwezenhs ordered Ahmek and Mudjeeka-wis out of the lodge.

"I'll call you when I want you," she said severely. "Scoot. Go. Now. Don't come back until I call."

A few hours later as they sat nibbling grass shoots on the dam, their sharp ears caught her voice from the lodge. When they came in, they found her curled happily around two small fur balls with open eyes. The kits were busy nursing. They looked sleepily at their father and his tall white friend and then got back to business.

Early the next morning, as soon as they had fed, the kits began to explore the lodge. They came to the edge of the slope leading to the lower platform. They paused there for a moment. Their noses twitched like mad at the smell of water. First one and then the other slid over the edge, and waddled and rolled and slid some more until they were on the lower level.

The three adult beavers watched with delight as the two little ones, not yet a day old, came to the edge of the main plunge hole. They peered and sniffed at the circle of dark water. One of them was smaller and faster than the other. Without warning, without so much as dipping a paw into it, he disappeared into the water with scarcely a splash and was gone. Ahmek and Kwezenhs leapt forward anxiously, but Mudjeekawis calmly raised a paw, wait. And sure enough, in less than a second the little fellow was on the surface again, his nose and eyes out of the water. He was actually swimming!

"That's One!" Kwezenhs said happily.

The plumper, slower one watched the first for a moment. Then, with a small plop! she, too, went over the edge.

"That's Two," Kwezenhs said.

Two dropped out of sight, surfaced a moment later, and swam around in circles with her brother, mewing happily, as the three adult beavers watched with love and fascination.

After a few minutes of this, the smaller kit, One, began to make sucking sounds and to look a little cross. He gazed hungrily at his mother. He tried to climb out of the plunge hole and managed to get his front paws partway up the slippery collar of the hole. But then he slid backwards with a splash, submerged, came up spluttering, and immediately began to cry.

Plump, easygoing Two swam in circles around her brother, watching his performance with what looked suspiciously like disapproval.

Kwezenhs went into the water with them and pushed both kits out of the water with her head, then nudged them up the slope to the upper platform the same way, and soon the two were contentedly feeding again, nuzzled close to their mother.

The second day she had them out of the lodge, into the pond, swimming beside her like tugboats guiding a supertanker out of the harbour.

Within a week, they were on shore nibbling on grasses. A week after that, as the first poplar buds began to appear, they were introduced to that delicacy, too. Kwezenhs kept feeding them as well. She would keep on doing this for almost a month.

It was June, now. Tasty fresh greens were bursting out of the ground in all directions. Winter was forgotten, the upside-down time under the ice. There was lots to eat and no work to do. Beavers like to play, and the kits and their mother played together day after day.

The kits began to give each other Messages. They supposed they were inventing this form of magical, silent communication. Their mother allowed them to believe this for the time being. She remembered when she was a kit. She knew that thinking this gift was unique to them gave them a sense of having their own special, private space.

After messaging they would dance and wrestle and fall in the water and climb out again and laugh and dance and wrestle again until they were out of breath or hungry — or both.

While the kits were playing around their mother, Ahmek set about digging canals and escape holes along the shore of Shinibeesh. He did this more for fun than anything else, but partly because it reminded him of Wiyaunuk and of his father and grandmother. At last he was able to think about them without feeling too sad, really, and he liked the memories to swirl around him as he dug and shovelled and tunnelled and built. As soon as he had a canal deep enough to use, he would bring the kits to it, push some small logs into the water in front of them, and guide them until their instincts kicked in. Then they began to push the little logs along the surface towards Shinibeesh and the dam just as if they had been doing it all their lives.

Wah-jusk the Muskrat was very busy with his new family, as well. He had proudly brought the four young muskrats swimming by for a visit when they were about ten days old — muskrats are born hairless and blind and have to be taught to swim. They are not as quick as beaver to navigate on their own. The good friends Ahmek and Wah-jusk were as fond of each other as ever, but now the old muskrat had an audience right in his own den. If the wind was in the right direction on some nights, when the beaver family was out foraging or just swimming back and forth, they could faintly hear Wah-jusk's reedy old voice singing story songs and lullabies until the young rats were asleep, and then love songs and ballads after that.

One and Two, the beaver kits, were growing fast. Already they had begun to feel confident and clever. Because nature has stored so many skills in the beavers' genes (instead of — as in the case of humans — giving them almost no skills but a huge capacity for learning stuff), it is not long before brand-new beavers start to act as if they have been around for a very long time. And to talk as if they know a great deal about everything.

So then they start to show off a bit. It is said that some very young humans also do this from time to time, but probably quite differently from beavers.

Young beavers are particularly inclined to show off their tail-splashing skills. The older beavers will watch this for a while, and then, when the showing off gets particularly outrageous and a young kit who weighs no more than five or six pounds surfaces after what it thinks is a splash the size of an earthquake, one of the adults will swim up beside the little one who is grinning all over with pride, and show the kit how a real beaver smacks the water. Just to let it know that, well, there are still a few things to learn in life.

Two was especially vain about her tail. She groomed it with extravagant care. She boasted — quite correctly, it must be admitted — that she could splash ever so much louder than her older brother (older by about one minute).

Sometimes her boasting and her endless tail slapping made One feel a bit sad. He would go off by himself and sulk. After watching this happen three or four times in a row, Kwezenhs swam up beside Two in the midst of one of her displays and made a splash the size of the seismic wave that wiped out the village of Moa Moa in the Philippines in 1897. This one turned the poor little kit over and over three or four times in its aftershocks, and then washed her up on shore. Two was bright enough to get the point and cool it a little with the showing off after that. But she remained very proud of her tail and her splashes.

Another thing beaver kits do that gets their parents pretty vexed is wander off without telling anyone.

Now, as we've seen, wandering is what beavers are genetically programmed to do. Almost all young beavers at the age of about two years leave the home colony and start their wander time, searching out new territory and new companions. Very young beavers, perhaps to practise for that trip they will inevitably be forced to take when they are adolescents, that is, two-year-olds, sometimes get the urge to wander off without telling anyone.

They usually get lost then, and the parents have to go looking for them. Probably the parents will find the kits curled up under a log somewhere, whimpering and scared.

Then there will be a lot of scolding from the parents, and tall tales from the kits about the terrible encounters they had with Wingizwaush the Osprey or Mukwoh the bear and how cleverly they outwitted the ferocious enemy and so on. By the time they get home to their Wiyaunuk or their Shinibeesh, everybody will be laughing again, and in a good mood, especially if they have found something really nice to eat on the way home — which they usually do.

Well, an evening came when One said to Two, "Let's go for a hike. Let's go downstream below the dam and see where it leads to." And without saying a thing to Ahmek or Kwezenhs, off they went.

But Mudjeekawis overheard them and saw them go. He sat on the dam and gazed thoughtfully after them for as much time as it takes the sun to move past a big old pine tree trunk. Then he submerged and swam along the bottom, cruising back and forth over the submarine landscape that he had come to know so well during the long winter under the ice. He passed a small school of speckled trout finning idly in the shadows under the north bank, but they did not speak to him and he did not speak to them.

He paused for a while by the underwater entrance to Wah-jusk and Tess's new den. Wah-jusk's head looked out. The grizzled old rodent saw something private and mysterious in the big white beaver's eyes, and after giving him a grave and respectful nod of greeting, he went back into his den again.

Mudjeekawis thought about that time when the muskrats' old den had frozen shut. He felt a sense of pride in the way his pupil, Ahmek, had led the rescue operation. He remembered with satisfaction how Ahmek had opened their own lodge's frozen plunge hole, how the young beaver had instantly understood his instructions and swiftly and surely set about butting open the ice at the top of the frozen plunge hole.

He chuckled silently at the memory of the invitation to eat with them, three times offered. And the invitation to stay the winter, also three times offered. He reflected with satisfaction on the way in which Ahmek now guided his children into the tasks they would need to be good at when it was their turn to tunnel and dig and build, and how warm and united the little family had become.

Mudjeekawis lifted his head out of the water and looked around the pond, the dam, the poplar stumps, the snug, round lodge with its fresh mudcap, the stone cliff rising in shadow now to the south.

"One generation passeth away and another generation cometh," he said softly. "But the Earth abideth forever."

He swam to the middle of the pond, slowed to a stop, and gazed at the darkening water. The sun was down. He found himself for a moment in the middle of a vision of the first winter of his own childhood, when a Human had found him shivering and hungry, cast away because of his colour, too young for a wander time, lonely and frightened. The Human had taken him home to a warm cabin and made him a big bath, and allowed him to sleep in the bed with him if he wanted to, and read to him by lamplight during the long winter nights, from big old books that smelled like the woods in autumn, and fed him apples and peanut butter (now his mouth watered a little remembering). When the summer came, the Human told the now very large and very confident white beaver that he belonged in the wild and must be brave, and that he must go and dream his own dreams and find his own way.

He remembered how that very night, already far from the Human's cabin, he had dreamed a waking dream, and Nanabush had visited him, if it really was Nanabush, a great soft light all around him, messaging him. A dream that gave him his mission: to teach, to guide and nurture and help, and always to wander.

"To every thing there is a season," Mudjeekawis whispered to himself, a little hoarsely. "A time to keep and a time to cast away. I have really stayed too long. Nanabush would not be pleased.

"Oh dear," he said to himself. "Sometimes it is hard to be a teacher."

He swam slowly towards the lodge.

"Children," he said, after squeezing the water from his fur with more than his usual solemnity. "Children, I must leave you."

Ahmek looked up sharply and was about to protest — three times if necessary. But Kwezenhs knew better. She signalled her mate to be silent. Mudjeekawis went on.

"Somewhere there is another young beaver wandering. Who needs my guidance. How I know these things I cannot tell you, but simply that the Message comes, and when it comes I must obey."

The three animals looked at each other solemnly for as long as it might take the sun to pass the trunks of two old pine trees. Then they rose and embraced each other, and stood close with their heads together. As always the Message had no words, though it was full of love and courage.

Now they sat on their tails, all three, a little away from each other, their eyes closed, to have a dream. Ahmek dreamed of N'Okomis. Kwezenhs dreamed of One and Two and felt vaguely uneasy.

When they opened their eyes, their old teacher was gone.

Ahmek suddenly had to clean his nose. He cleaned it for a long time, rather noisily, coughing and huffing as he did so, with his back to Kwezenhs.

Just as he was finishing this task, the water in the plunge hole heaved and subsided and heaved again and a big white head emerged.

"Ahem," Mudjeekawis said. "I forgot to tell you. The kits have gone downstream. Towards the big river.

They will be all right. I believe you should wait until tomorrow, till the deep purple falls."

"What?" said Kwezenhs.

"When the stars begin to twinkle in the sky," Mudjeekawis hummed. "By then they will be very glad to see you. I predict that you will find them in an abandoned Mukwoh den, quite close to the big river, on the north side of the stream. Good-bye now."

And he was gone again.

SIXTEEN   *Black Canoes Again*

Exactly as Mudjeekawis had foreseen, the frightened kits were huddled, whimpering, in a halfcollapsed bear's winter den on the side of the hill almost within sight of the big river. After a bit of ritual scolding, which nobody took very seriously, and much hugging and sniffling and licking and smelling each other, One and Two were able to stop sobbing and tell of their adventure.

"A huge Kookookoo came down out of the sky and tried to eat us!" Two said. "But we jumped into the stream and I slapped my tail so hard I sent water flying into the air, all over the huge bird. It went Hoo! HOO! and flew away."

"Are you sure it was a Kookookoo?" Ahmek asked. "Big round eyes? Did it come in the night?"

"Yes! Yes!" they both said at once. "Just the way you

warned us to watch out for."

"It flew away after I yelled at it," One said. "I yelled as loud as I could and I scared it away."

"OH, and there were Mukwoh all around," Two said. "When we heard them growling we jumped into the stream and stayed underwater as long as we could. Then we just put our eyes and noses out, like this, and if they were gone we came out. And if they were still looking for us we went under again. I can stay under much longer than One."

"Did you actually see the Mukwoh?"

"Well, no. But we heard them. All around us. Growling, grrrr, like that."

"But the most terrible thing is the black logs and the tall animals that make lights on the ground," One said, very mysteriously. "Huge big animals with clouds coming out of their noses and lights on their paws, and black logs they sit inside of."

"Hmmm," Ahmek thought. "Now this sounds like a different kind of story." Suddenly he was very interested.

"Where did you see these big animals with their black logs?"

"We went to the end of the stream," Two said. "One is telling the truth, really. At the end of the stream, guess what? There is a big water. Bigger than Shinibeesh. So big it doesn't need a dam. On the far side there is a flat place. The big animals were floating in their logs near the flat place. They climbed out of their black logs and then guess what. They pulled their black logs up onto the flat place!"

Ahmek said, "And then they made clouds come out of sticks on the ground?"

Two was surprised. "You were watching us all the time," she said bitterly, afraid her story and her surprises were all in vain.

"No, no," Ahmek said, "We didn't know where you were. We were very worried. Now, we know you are brave and we were sure that you would look after yourself, but . . . ." He was remembering a terrible time of his own.

"So how did you know about the clouds coming out of the sticks on the ground?"

"One and Two," Ahmek said proudly, "You may have discovered something very important. Can you take us to where those big animals are?"

The beaver family went downstream by water. Soon they clambered over the rocks where the brook tumbled and gurgled into the big river. On the far shore they could easily make out the faint orange glow. There was a grey angular shape near the sticks. All these things were some distance away, across the wide river. Ahmek wanted a closer look. He was tense and alert and angry. But he was not afraid.

Kwezenhs agreed that the family would wait for him by the outfall of the little brook, right where Lawren Harris and Jim MacDonald and Alex Jackson had met the poachers. Ahmek, of course, knew nothing about that episode. He plunged into the water and swam silently towards the far shore. A few body lengths out he stopped and sniffed and stared at the land. He was close enough to hear the Humans breathing in their sleep and making strange rumbling noises. The Humans were inside the grey anuglar shape Ahmek had seen from across the river. The shape had flaps on the water side, and some long lines, like vines, held it up to the trees near it.

On the ground, near the still glowing, smoking sticks, there were some black shapes, round, with a few shiny edges, and another shiny thing that you could see through that seemed to have a little reddish swamp water in the bottom of it. Ahmek could tell from the sound of the Humans that they were very deeply asleep.

He saw with interest that there was a tall, old, heavy poplar growing on a slant, leaning over the tattered shelter where the Humans were sleeping. One of the vines, or roots — some kind of stringy thing that held up the shelter — was fastened to this huge poplar. Ahemk grimly recognized the two black logs. He remembered the dirty, sour smell of these Humans. He swam back across the river to his waiting family.

"How would you like . . .?" he began, solemnly.

"Well?" asked Kwezenhs.

"How would you like . . ." Ahmek repeated, looking quite cheerful and excited all of a sudden, "how would you like to help me cut down a really big tree?"

The two kits promised to stay put. They watched curiously as their parents swam quietly across the river, climbed out on the flat rock near the black logs and approached the base of the ancient poplar.

The far shore was too distant for the kits to hear the gnawing sounds, but from time to time in the starlight they caught the gleam of a white chip being torn away from the trunk.

Ahmek and Kwezenhs worked on opposite sides of the tree. It was far bigger than anything they had ever cut before. They had many times given up on smaller trees. But now they chewed and tore away at the trunk without resting, although from time to time their instincts made them stop and listen for sounds of danger.

When they were about halfway through the trunk, the tree became weakened by their cutting and shifted suddenly under its own massive weight. With a loud scraping noise its branches brushed across those of a neighbouring white pine, high above them. The snoring in the tent stopped. A voice said, "Whazzat? Whazzat?" Another voice said, "Shaddup, shaddup."

A head poked out of the tent flap and looked around. The beavers froze. The head was followed by a pair of shoulders. One of the men came out of the tent and walked to the fire. He did not look towards the tree, but went to the other side of the campsite and leaned against another tree. The beavers could hear a trickle of running water. It did not make them want to build. The man came back towards the fire, bent down, picked up a bottle, sniffed at it — empty — puffed a disgusted sound, and threw the bottle into the river. He shuffled back to the tent, scuffling bright new poplar chips under his feet as he went without even noticing them. He muttered crossly and disappeared back into the tent.

The beavers waited. After what seemed a very long time snoring began again. Ahmek and Kwezenhs began to cut wood again.

They did not have to work very long. The old poplar, rotten at the core and already leaning precariously, began to make a groaning, cracking sound. Ahmek and

Kwezenhs jumped clear. They raced to the rocky edge and dived in with a loud splash, no point being silent now.

Two and a half tons of wood came crashing down like thunder, like the sky falling, like a comet colliding with a planet.

Now as we have already seen, although their engineering skills are truly remarkable, beavers are not brilliant when it comes to felling trees where they want them to go. The falling poplar just missed the tent.

It hit the canoes instead. Well, one canoe, to be accurate. A big branch, broken off to a sharp point as it careered past the neighbouring white pine on the way down, pierced the bottom of the second canoe right through the keel like a huge skewer, spoiling it for any future use. The tent rope tied to the tree trunk was drawn tight as a piano wire when the massive trunk rolled two or three times on its way down. The rope did not break. It pulled the tent down flat, wrapping the four men inside into a bundle like sausages in vacuum-wrap in the supermarket, although, of course, vacuum-wrapped sausages would not be invented for another forty years.

There was a stunned silence for about as long as it takes a beaver to reach the bottom of the river, where Kwezenhs and Ahmek had swiftly dived when the comet hit the planet.

By the time they surfaced again, gingerly, for a look-see, the tent had turned into a very large, lumpy, dirty white flatfish, flapping and bulging and straining to escape the lines that held it relentlessly to the ground. The beavers watched and listened, not understanding the words but enjoying their message.

"I'm suffocatin'!" a voice called desperately, muffled, from inside the fish. "My knife! My knife!" another voice choked out. "Where the devil is my knife?"

"Ow! Ow! It's stickin' into my bum, you dimwit," another muffled voice said. "Here, hold on, stop wrigglin'. Stop! Stop!" There was a brief silence.

"There!" a voice said. There was ripping sound. A head appeared through the side of the tent. The four drunken, scared poachers clambered through the slit, gulping for air, cursing and groaning. They raced around the campsite confusedly, trying to figure out what had happened. Suddenly sobered they gathered around the astonishing evidence at the base of the old poplar.

"Sheesh!" one of them whispered, in awe. "That ain't no ordinary beaver."

"I don't like this," another said.

There was a brief silence.

"I don't know about you guys," a voice said. "But I'm gettin' the hell outta here. I don't like this. It ain't natural."

"Know what I think?" another said. "Remember that painter we beat up on last summer? I always thought he'd try to get back at us. Maybe he sneaks up, tryin' to make us think it was a beaver. No beaver gonna do that. We catch that son of a . . ."

There was no point trying to rescue the tent or its contents. They took the minimum. They clambered into the one remaining serviceable black canoe. It sank almost to the gunwales. Still cursing and muttering, but careful not to rock the boat, they started gingerly paddling. They veered crazily this way and that in the dark channel as the whisky asserted itself again, but they went more or less north, towards Joe Lake.

SEVENTEEN   *Wiyaunuk Again?*

The summer deepened, and the South Wind smote the beavers with his heat. Mostly they came out at night to eat. Even in the shady dome of the lodge it was uncomfortably hot from mid-morning till well after sunset.

The kits, who had promised faithfully not to wander any more without warning, grew rapidly. One night a violent thunderstorm brought all the water in the western hemisphere down on their little valley. In only a few hours the level of Shinibeesh rose rapidly and washed away part of the dam. Then the kits fell to with their parents, cutting sticks and bringing mud and building away like, well, like beavers. They did not have to be told to do this; they just did it.

As always when mending dam, Ahmek thought fondly of N'Osse and N'Okomis, and even occasionally of his mother, although that thought was still painful. One evening as they emerged from the lodge after an afternoon sleep and came up on the north end of the dam to enjoy the last rays of the sun, Kwezenhs sensed that Ahmek's mind was somewhere else. She stood up in front of him and indicated that she wanted to message.

They stood with their paws on each other's shoulders for a few minutes, rocking gently back and forth. Presently Kwezenhs said, "Well then, why don't we go there, and see for ourselves?"

"What!" said Ahmek. He had not been aware how full his thoughts were of Wiyaunuk.

"Look," said Kwezenhs. "It's different for me. I left my home pond because it was time to leave. I was ready. I left with good messages all round, and good friends, and no pain and no worry. You were forced to leave. You are still worried about them, aren't you? Well, maybe it would be safe to go and have a look. We wouldn't have to stay there if there's nothing to stay for. Shinibeesh will look after itself for a few days. Do you think you could find Wiyaunuk?"

"Oh, I could find it all right," Ahmek said. "But those Humans in the black log, they went that way I think. And they were pretty angry, and . . ."

"Ahmek?"

"What?" he said, a bit irritably.

"Ahmek," she said tolerantly, "why don't we sleep on it?"

And they went for a swim in the soft summer night.

Ahmek had a dream. Mudjeekawis stood in the moonlight. He said, "The Kitchi Manitou has sent a great fear, a Zaegiziwin, upon the Black Logs. They have gone far away to escape the Zaegiziwin. They will not come back. It is time for you to take a trip to the north, Ahmek. Go north by water."

The white shape faded away. Ahmek woke up slowly and thought about it. Kwezenhs said, "I dreamed of Mudjeekawis, Ahmek. He said, 'Go north.'"

They had dreamed the same dream.

They swam around Shinibeesh, looking at all the wonderful things they had built. "See?" Kwezenhs reassured him. "Everything's in good shape. The dam is strong, the lodge is tight. There's nothing we have to do. We have all summer ahead of us. Everything will still be here when we come back. Let's do it. You'll keep on fretting if we don't."

She had a practical mind, Kwezenhs.

They came to Wah-jusk's den. Jolly songs and laughter rang from within. They blew bubbles and scratched at the entrance until the muskrats came to see who was there. Ahmek told them that he and Kwezenhs and the kits were going to be away for a while, and why.

"Well now, you know me," Wah-jusk said. "I'm a stick in the mud. Really. I like my home mud. Not much fer travel. Specially these days. Young family keeps a fella at home, ya know? But I hear you talkin' plenty since we knew each other. Talkin' about yer folks, how you miss them. So, yeah, maybe you should go. I'll keep an eye on the place. Any unwelcome customers come along, I'll do some voices, scare 'em away. Count on me. Don't worry about a thing.

"I'll miss ya, though," he added. "Well," chuckling,

looking fondly at Tess, "Guess I'll get along okay."

 ⚏

They travelled mostly by night, resting whenever the kits began to slow down.

First they went downstream, over the little burbling water at stream's end and into the deep river. Kwezenhs and Ahmek took the kits over to see the broken black log. They all looked with awe at the wreckage of the huge tree and the sodden remains of the tattered grey shelter and its filthy contents.

Then the four beavers plunged excitedly into the big river again and struck off northward in the lovely night. At first they kept close to shore, in the safety of shadows. Later, as they became accustomed to the big water, they often swam right out in mid-river, pleased by the expanse of water all around them. North, Mudjeekawis had said in the dream.

At dawn they came ashore and had a good feed. Then they built a rough shelter and slept most of the sunny hours, in the shade but never very far from water.

On the third night they were swimming strongly up the west shore, where the river had widened out considerably. In fact, it had become a lake.

"This might be Zaaghigan, the big lake," Ahmek said to Kwezenhs. "We may be getting close!"

There were many little islands in the lake. The navigation was tricky. Ahmek moved his little flotilla across to the shadows close to the east side of the lake.

Suddenly he stopped. He held his nose high in the

air like a pyramid. A low bank of fog was rolling out of a narrow bay off to the right. A familiar scent came down with the fog, swampy, strong. That scent tugged at Ahmek's heartstrings.

"We're here," Ahmek said. "We're here!"

They turned eastward into the narrow bay and into the fog. At the end of the bay the fog lifted. There was a slow, shallow stream. They waded up its bed and clambered over stones and fallen tree trunks, heading east, deep into the forest. Ahmek's heart was beating fast. The shape of things was getting very familiar.

After an hour they heard water running. It sounded like water running over a ledge, perhaps through a break in a dam. It came closer, that sound, as they went up. It was terribly dark. The sound of running water was right ahead of them now. Their paws began to twitch with the urge to build.

Ahmek looked up. He saw a broad, dark, familiar mass of mud and sticks and stones.

It was Okwanim.

By now, it was the dark of the moon; so even though beavers can do a great deal by smell and feel, it was hard to get a sense of what kind of shape Wiyaunuk was in. Not much different, Ahmek thought, from that last terrible night he had spent here, however long ago. There seemed nothing to do but yield to the twitching in their paws and work through the night. At sunrise they would be able to see how the pond was.

So they began to repair Okwanim. The four of them went hard at it for the rest of the night.

By the time the first light began to show grey against the tangle of spruce at the east end of

Wiyaunuk, the flow was stopped and the broad gap
that had let the pond run off into the forest was almost
closed. The repair work rose well above the surface of
the little basin at the foot of the breach, the basin
where Ahmek had struggled with the dog and where
his father had barely missed being trapped alive. They
could rest now. All four beavers made scented mud pies,
on different parts of the dam. It was the first time that
One and Two had done this.

As the features of the pond emerged from darkness
with the advancing dawn Ahmek could see that almost
nothing had changed except for a growth of swampy
grasses over most of what had once been the bottom of
the pond. There was the lodge, he saw, looking a little
sad and caved in, over there by the south shore. He
could see one of the entrance holes too. And there was
the indentation of an escape hole in the bank. He
remembered that escape hole. There was the old main
canal leading up towards West Zaudeek. The canal was
dry and thickly overgrown with beaver grass, cattails,
moss, marsh marigolds, and other flowers.

Ahmek led his little family into the escape tunnel.
It was the same one he had hidden in the night of the
disaster. A few body lengths away from the bank, part
of the tunnel had caved in. It took only a few minutes
to clear away the rubble and pack the walls and the
ceiling, and then they all settled down to sleep through
the hottest part of the day.

By late afternoon they were rested and awake and
excited again. The repairs to Okwanim were already
showing results. Water was spreading back across the
grassy flats of the old pond bottom. It had not reached

the old family lodge yet, but Ahmek was sure that it would soon. He brought his new family to see the old homestead. They all crawled up the dry and dusty outer plunge hole, looked over the damage, and started to work on it as well.

All this was not so much a thought-out plan as a deep and irresistible urge.

They put fresh sticks in the weak part of the roof and packed it with a thick layer of mud. They swept out all the old bark and broken twigs and dry dirt and brought in a fresh supply of shaved bark and dry grass to sleep on. By the end of their second night's work, the lodge was livable again. As soon as the water rose above the lower openings of the tunnels, they would be able to move in.

That next afternoon they were awakened early by water lapping at the entrance to their sleeping place in the escape tunnel. By the time a thin crescent moon began to show through the trees to the west, water was almost at the lower entrance to the lodge.

The four beavers were pleased with their work. They took a break and ambled up the still dry canal bed to the poplars at West Zaudeek. There they gave themselves a good feed.

Two days later they were able to move into the lodge. After the kits were asleep Kwezenhs and Ahmek talked about what it all meant.

"How do you feel now?" she asked him.

"I think . . . I think I don't want to stay here much longer, if that's what you mean," Ahmek answered slowly. "I know it seems a bit strange to repair a dam and a lodge and watch the pond fill up, to — you know

— go to all that trouble and then just leave it. But I *had* to bring it back to the way it was, you know. And now that I've done that, I guess I have to admit that it is all over for me here. We belong at Shinibeesh. Shinibeesh is our place. We made it. I would like to play here for a few more days, just remembering, you know? And then I'll be ready to . . . ."

Ahmek looked warmly at his mate. "I was going to say, 'to go home,' wasn't I? Home is Shinibeesh now. I realize that. This place seems to be only a memory now."

"My Ahmek," was all that Kwezenhs said.

Ahmek awoke from his afternoon nap feeling restless. The family was still sound asleep. Slowly, so as not to wake them, he slipped into the plunge hole, dived to the bottom, and surfaced. He smelled a familiar scent. A voice from the water behind him said, "Coming out to play?"

"Ningik! Oh Ningik! Where did you come from?"

The otter grinned at his old friend. Both of them were remembering all those times when Ningik had come up that hole to see if his friend would come out to play. Ningik's muzzle had a little touch of grey to it. He said, "I live down in Zaaghigan now, Ahmek. I've got a family, three little ones and a lot of relatives from the west country. I am afraid they don't have quite the same feelings about beavers that I do, so . . . . But I was swimming by that part of the narrow bay where the stream comes out, and there was no water flowing in it, and I wondered if someone was building a dam again in Wiyaunuk. I came up to Okwanim and smelled your mud pie. And some other ones too. And here you are. Now listen. Guess what?"

Ningik's eyes were bright with excitement. It was clear he had a lot more to say. Ahmek headed for the plunge hole and out into Wiyaunuk so they could chat without waking the family. He did not want Kwezenhs to wake up and find an otter in her house, at least not before the somewhat unusual friendship had been explained. He had never told her that his closest boyhood companion was a member of an enemy tribe.

"Well," Ningik said. "There *is* someone I want you to . . . ah . . . meet. But it'll take me a day to arrange it. I'll be back tomorrow afternoon. Okay?" And he scampered up over the dam, down into the stream beyond, and was gone. Ahmek crossed the pond and climbed out on shore, on a flat place where there were still some charred sticks and black stones arranged in a circle. He sat there in the late sun, enjoying its warmth, and wondering who it was Ningik would come back with.

Kwezenhs and the kits came out before sunset. Once they had bathed and oiled Ahmek took them for a long, easygoing swim around Wiyaunuk, now close to its old level again. He told them stories about his childhood there, about the friendly Human and the Round Ones, about the fight with the strange, four-legged animal, even about the sad time when his own mother had gone out to repair Okwanim and was never seen again.

Kwezenhs did not like the children to hear that story, but Ahmek thought it was just as well for the kits to know how serious this question of human beings and their strange ways could be.

The next afternoon Ahmek woke up early. He felt restless. He decided to wait for Ningik at the old campsite. Leaving the others sleeping in the lodge, he swam underwater across Wiyaunuk, almost touching the grassy bottom. As the bottom sloped up towards the shore he passed over a small, rusted blade, half-buried in the bottom clay but with its handle sticking up, and a touch of red still on the handle. Closer to the bank, floating but lodged in a crack in a stone, he saw a flat piece of wood with some coloured marks on it. The colours showed faintly through a layer of green slime that had formed on the board. Ahmek took it with his teeth and brought it up onto the flat ground. He nibbled at it but it tasted terrible, strong turpentine and bitter oils.

He lay comfortably in the warm sunlight. He dozed off thinking about the friendly Human and N'Okomis and the taste and smell of Round Ones.

"What a realistic dream!" he thought. Still half-asleep, he could smell familiar beaver smells. He could hear a familiar chuckling sound.

Suddenly he knew it was not a dream. His skin felt cold with a strange emotion. He was afraid to open his eyes.

He opened his eyes.

A big, grizzled, plump old beaver face was staring at him, inches from his own. The old beaver was chuckling and weeping at the same time. It was an old lady beaver.

"N'Okomis!" Ahmek said. Behind her he saw another old beaver. "N'Osse! My father!" For some time he could not say anything else. There was much muzzling and mewing before anyone could speak.

Then N'Osse and N'Okomis told their story. Ningik stayed politely in the background, but listened.

When the family fled Wiyaunuk that dreadful night, Ahmek had headed south, but N'Osse and N'Okomis had gone north. They had travelled without stopping until they could travel no more. They crossed a strange flat place with long straight lines of some hard, hard material, which gleamed in the moonlight. Fearfully, they had watched the thunder spirit, huge and black and smoking, race along those lines. They had gone to a big lake beyond the thunder spirit lines, where they met some friendly beavers and joined a colony and built themselves a little lodge in a quiet backwater.

"Now, Ahmek," said his father. "There is something else." N'Osse looked at his son in a very special way. "There is someone here to see you. Waiting at Okwanim. We thought that would be the best place. You swim over there and you'll see."

Ahmek looked sharply at his father and at N'Okomis. They looked back at him with twinkling eyes and secret smiles. What were they up to now, those two?

A bit cross with all this secrecy, he leapt into the water with a noisy splash and swam as fast as he could towards the dam.

Even before he got there he could see yet another beaver. A biggish beaver, though not as big as N'Okomis. The big beaver was standing tall, her tail forward between her legs. She was standing just above the newly repaired breach in the dam. In the last low slanting rays of the sun, the edges of her ears gleamed silver.

"Mother," Ahmek mewed. For a moment his voice sounded just like a kit's.

EIGHTEEN   *Silvertips's Story*

There was a long, delirious, unbelievable time of
nothing but nuzzling and mewing and licking and
embracing and messages and rocking and laughing and
weeping and rocking again. Then N'Osse and N'Okomis
felt it would be all right for them to join in, and the nuzzling and mewing and messages started all over again.
The crescent moon, now a little higher and a little thicker as the night fell, showed three pairs of ripple lines
coming across the pond towards Okwanim. Kwezenhs
and the kits. The three of them climbed up on the dam.
Kwezenhs hung back, feeling shy for once in her life.
But the kits rushed forward, full of curiosity.

Silvertips gathered them up in her big front paws.
"I am your N'Okomis," she said. And then she greeted
Kwezenhs with a long, quiet Message.

And then it was time to tell her story.

"Now, I had been warned. I had been warned a lot," Silvertips said. "Just as I warned you, Ahmek, about the scent of Humans. I really knew better. Or perhaps we beavers never *do* know better when the water is rushing through a hole in the dam, I'm not sure.

"Well. You three had gone off to cut logs. I said to myself, I should wait for them to come back before I go into the breach. But the water was rushing so loud, the pond was going down so fast, I had to begin. I couldn't help it. And, Bang! A great clanging thing closed on me. I was in a big box. I could see through its sides. They were like hard strings, or thin, thin, criss-crossed branches when we are building a lodge. But when I tried to bite through them I broke off part of a tooth. Too hard. *Very* hard! And I was underwater, and the thing was heavy. I believed I was going to drown. But suddenly I was lifted out. By — Oh, Ahmek! It was awful. By *Humans*! Their smell was . . . . Well, it was the worst thing I ever smelled in my life.

"But frightened as I was, I was glad they ran off with me before you came back. At least, I thought — at least my family is safe.

"They put me in their floating log. Then they moved me into a dark, closed wooden box. There were only tiny air holes, and nothing to drink or to wash in. Then it was quiet for a long time. Then . . . Ahmek, you remember the strange thunder?"

N'Osse said, "We have told him we saw the thunder spirit smoking along the shining lines in the forest."

"Yes! Well!" said Silvertips. "After that long, quiet wait I could hear the voices of humans and I could hear the thunder coming. It came so close I felt I was inside it. Then suddenly I really was inside it. *I was inside the thunder spirit!* The whole world was full of thunder noises.

"So. Do you know what I did? I began to cut wood, to chew away at the sides of the box. It is hard to try cutting through a flat surface when you can't get your teeth *around* something. But I kept on.

"It was very hard wood, and it tasted terrible. It had pieces of those hard strings that broke my tooth, all through it. But I cut and I cut. Somehow, I managed to tear out the hard strings, to tear them away from the wood. After a very long time I broke through. But then I saw that I was in an even bigger wooden box, a huge box, very dark, full of other smaller boxes, and the thunder all around, and the whole thing shaking and making such dreadful, dreadful noises!

"After a while the thunder became softer and slower. The shaking stopped. Everything got quiet. I was afraid they would come for me. I hid behind some boxes.

"The side of the big box opened up. Cool air came in. I could smell the forest outside, but it wasn't our forest, it was a strange forest. I could hear Human voices. Some Humans came into the big box. They brought other boxes. They went out. They came back with more boxes. I waited until they seemed far away, then I jumped. I hurt my leg falling down, but I was free.

"But, Ahmek, I had no idea where I was. I was a very, very long way from Wiyaunuk. That is all I knew. I hid and watched until the giant black thunder spirit started to smoke again and it went away.

"I said to myself, 'Well, I better go the other way. I'll follow its tracks back to where it came from.' Well. It was much longer than my wander year, I can tell you. I travelled every day. My feet got very sore sometimes and I would have to rest. Sometimes, would you believe this? Sometimes it would be days and days and days without any water to bathe in. My tail got dry, the skin on it cracked. I was bleeding. But I knew, deep inside me, I must follow the thunder spirit's tracks. More thunder spirits came along. Perhaps it was the same one coming and going. I would hide in the woods.

"It was getting cold. I had to dig a little lodge, just a cave in a river bank, and cut winter food. All alone. I was very hungry that winter. I believed I was dying. Nanabush came in a dream. I am sure it was Nanabush. 'Keep on,' Nanabush said. 'Keep on.'

"I passed a number of colonies. Some kind beavers invited me to stay. One chap . . . . Well . . . ." Silvertips here looked sideways at N'Osse. N'Osse looked at the sky and rocked a little. But he was really smiling.

"A very nice chap, really — an older chap — asked me to move in with him. I was tired of travel, and I was lonely, and I was very tempted. But I thought of my dream. 'Keep on.' So I kept on.

"Then I came to a colony that seemed more like our beavers. And you know, I was tired. So tired of travelling. I had begun to lose hope about ever getting home, and it was so nice to feel I could rest among friends. So I thought, 'I'll stay here for a while and get my strength back.'

"Well, there were actually some of my relatives there. And one girl from my home colony, a girl who had gone on her wander year the same time as I did, and we remembered each other. I settled down with them. And then, just when I was thinking it was time to get on the move again, to try to find my way back to Wiyaunuk, your father and N'Okomis showed up, and told me the story of how you all left Wiyaunuk. Of course, we thought we would never see you again.

"Now, I don't like to ever say anything good about otters. And you can be sure if I hadn't been taken away by those terrible Humans you would not have been allowed to grow up playing with an otter every day, Ahmek, I don't know what your grandmother was thinking.

"However, I have to admit, well, *I* can't do it, but I hope you will say thank you to Ningik for me. Because he did bring us back together again, didn't he?"

Ahmek glanced across the water towards a familiar half-sunk log. He thought he saw a familiar shape crouched there, and two small eyes faintly gleaming. He knew that otters have very sharp ears.

NINETEEN   *Now*

They talked all night. In the morning, before it got too hot, they took a tour around Wiyaunuk, all together, to see the work that had been done. If you had been watching from a secret place on the shore of the pond you would have seen the amazing sight of seven sets of beaver wakes all at once, going to the canal (now full again), to the escape holes, to the lodge, back to the dam.

N'Osse said proudly, "I thought I was the master builder. But you four have done a fine job. A fine job. Thank you. It will be so nice to move back into our old home again. And, Ahmek, you can build a lodge with Kwezenhs and One and Two, right over there, by the east shore. I have always thought that would make a fine situation for a lodge. Don't you think so too?"

Ahmek looked affectionately at his father. The old

beaver was beginning to look old, not as old as N'Okomis, but getting on. Time for some peace and quiet in his life, not to be troubled by youngsters scrapping and yelling and tearing around. And, anyway, Ahmek and Kwezenhs had already talked it over. They knew where home was for them.

"Well now," Ahmek said. He looked affectionately at his father. "Ah, I think we'll be heading back to Shinibeesh," he said kindly. "And we'll tell you exactly how to find us. Whenever you feel like a visit you'll come. It's a three-day trip by water. A nice trip. And we will come and visit you. And when One and Two go on their wander year some time, they'll come by and say hello. We'll all be just fine.

"Only watch out for black logs," Ahmek added. "Well, actually," he remembered, "I have had a good dream." And he told the whole story of his big white friend Mudjeekawis, and finally of the last dream and the message about the Black Log Humans and the Zaegiziwin, the great fear that drove the bad Humans away.

"There will always be danger", N'Osse said. "That is part of beaver life. It is part of human life as well. Yesterday we crossed the big lake, Zaaghigan, mostly under water. We saw a drowned Human, Ahmek. With hard strings wrapped around his legs. On the bottom. We thought, perhaps, he looked like the kind Human, the one who gave us Round Ones that time, remember? And fought with the bad Humans? There is danger everywhere, Ahmek. So always be alert. Travel by night. Repair the dam. That is what beavers do."

Ahmek, of course, knew all that. Except the sad

story about the drowned Human. He hoped it wasn't the kind Human. But he knew about dangers, and he knew he would be giving lessons like this to One and Two before they left to make their own lives, to find their own Wiyaunuks and Shinibeeshes, meet their own mates, build their own lodges. "I am a N'Osse now," Ahmek said to himself.

He thought, "It would be nice for One and Two to have a N'Okomis to grow up with. But, of course, my mother must stay with my father, so it can't be her."

He turned to his old grandmother. "N'Okomis," he said. "Come with us. I want you to see our new lodge. I want you to stay with us for a while, maybe for the winter. I want you to tell stories to the kits and laugh with us. Will you do that?"

N'Okomis looked at N'Osse. "I think that would be a very good idea," N'Osse said. So it was agreed.

Ahmek went back into the pond and swam to where Ningik the Otter had waited patiently on a familiar old deadhead, diving to the bottom occasionally, to search for crayfish, more for something to do than because he was hungry.

Ahmek told his old friend all about the journey south, the spectral white beaver in the night, meeting Kwezenhs, the kits, the adventure with the lynx, the ice, Wah-jusk. Ningik boasted about his wonderful trio of youngsters, their swimming prowess, the great fishing in Zaaghigan. He thought it best not to say too much about his larger family, who, sadly, were as interested in catching beavers as they were in catching fish. Ahmek noticed the silence on that subject.

"Ningik," Ahmek said. "It's too bad we can't be

young again. When it didn't seem to matter that our families are enemies. My mother said to thank you, by the way, for bringing us back together again."

"I know," Ningik said. "I heard."

Ahmek said, "I thought so. I could see you on the deadhead."

"Well," the otter said, "I guess we have to be what we have to be and do what we have to do. But we had great times, didn't we, you and I?"

"We did, yes. We did. Well . . . good-bye, Ningik," Ahmek said quietly. "You are right. We have to be what we have to be, and that is all right."

He swam back to his family on the dam. There was another journey to be made.

☖

Reader, put on your giant dragonfly wings again. Rise up for one last look over these woods and lakes and ponds — just one. This is what you will see.

It is only the fourth night since the new crescent moon first sent silver light down on Wiyaunuk as Ahmek and his family began their splendid job of repairing the dam and the lodge. Now it is the half-moon, so there is quite a bit of light. If you peer carefully, you can see quite a lot. So much has happened, so many stories have been told, tears shed, laughter, embraces, mewings, messages.

Rise up above the treetops. Look south. There is Shinibeesh. If you are high enough, you can just make out the dark north face of the rocky cliff where Wah-jusk and Ahmek climbed for berries, from where they looked down with surprise at the arrival of a new beaver in the new pond. It was not so long ago, you know, but it seems long because so much has happened. Try listening. Maybe you can hear a thin, reedy old muskrat voice. Maybe it is singing a lullaby or a ballad.

If your eyes are really sharp, to the west of Shinibeesh, you can see a campsite on the bank of the big river, with a very big poplar on it, an old poplar newly felled. Perhaps the moonlight is glinting on its silvery old trunk.

You will have to be really sharp-eyed to see this at night, but you may be able to make out the heads of a pair of older beavers, just two of them, on Wiyaunuk, swimming easily, comfortably, lazily, around the pond their young Ahmek has fixed up so nicely for them.

Now move a little south, about halfway between Wiyaunuk and Shinibeesh. Look down towards the west again, to where Zaaghigan narrows into the river. You'll have to look closely. There! In the shadows! See? Hugging the shore for safety, but steaming along in convoy, there are four — no, by Nanabush! — there are *five* wakes moving along together. One of them is quite a wide wake. Can you hear anything? Can you hear a voice saying, "It might be nice, Ahmek, to stop and have a little snack, and then a little nap"? Can you hear that?

Look for one more thing, before you sink softly back to earth again. Look all over, in the woods, in the glades, the swamps, the beaches, on the river banks, beside the ponds. Maybe you will catch a little flash of white, gliding along through the woods, or pausing at the top of a slope to peer down, and around, looking for

. . . well, what is he looking for? Maybe you will catch a glimpse of this pale shape gliding. Or maybe you will just imagine it. Maybe you will imagine that you see it coming to a high ledge of rock, where it looks down upon five beaver wakes in convoy, heading south in the shadows for safety.

Maybe, in your imagination, you will hear it speak. Maybe it will be saying, softly to itself: "One generation passeth away, and another generation cometh. But the Earth abideth forever."

Maybe you will hear these words, or maybe you won't. But they are being spoken. Very good words, too. Whether you are a beaver or an otter. Or even a Human.

FIN

AFTERWORD

Like Ahmek himself, this book has a N'Osse and a Silvertips, a N'Okomis and a N'Mishomiss. That is, parents and grandparents in the form of other books. These are books that I loved when I was a boy and read again with a lot of pleasure even now. First among them is *The Sword in the Stone* by T. H. White. It's a little book about the legendary King Arthur, when he was a boy. It grew into a very big book called *The Once and Future King*. But *The Sword in the Stone* is the best part.

Then there was my first beaver story, *Flat Tail*, by Alice Crew Gall and Fleming Gall. It's still in my local public library and still a fine tale. (No pun.) And, of course, the great classics, *The Wind in the Willows* by Kenneth Grahame, and the Winnie the Pooh books by A. A. Milne.

And if you like intense books about the real life of animals, *Tarka the Otter*, by Henry Williamson, is pretty amazing.

I read all of these when I was a boy. They still echo in my mind. And they echo in *Ahmek*; if you liked *Ahmek*, I bet you'll like them, too.

The painter Tom Thomson is very real. He was one of the most original of a group of Ontario painters whose influence on how Canadians see their land has been huge. His friends, A. Y. Jackson ("Alex" in this book), J. E. H. MacDonald ("Jim"), and Lawren Harris, formed The Group of Seven, whose paintings are in many Canadian art galleries. Tom Thomson and Jim MacDonald really did paint at Canoe Lake, where Tom Thomson died mysteriously, in the lake, when he was only forty.

And this writer really did have that experience with the fog bank, where he thought for a moment that the famous Ghost of Tom Thomson was paddling beside him.

A NOTE ON THE LANGUAGE

Ojibway is perhaps the best known name of the
language spoken over vast areas of our continent
by the Anishinaabe people. For many of them it is
their first language, and many others are regaining
their roots by studying it as a second language. A small
number of other people, whose first language is not
Ojibwa, are also learning this rich and complex language
as a way of better knowing the origins of their wood-
land culture.

Mme Elaine Brant, a professional teacher of
Ojibway, has read the book and corrected the vocabu-
lary in places where some of the older forms, derived
from Bishop Frederic Baraga's dictionary (Montreal,
1878-1880), are no longer in use.

There are some dialect and regional variants in
both spelling and pronunciation. So if a word does not

look exactly like the version you may know, that may be the reason. The most modern spellings are from the 1993 publication, *Eastern Ojibwa-Chippewa-Ottawa Dictionary* by Richard Rhodes, published in Berlin and New York by Mouton de Gruyter. Some of these are difficult, and I have preferred older versions.

GLOSSARY

Aabidag: Certainly, it must be so

Ahmik (pl. Ahmikook): Beaver

Bboon: Winter

Bezhen: Lynx

Bimidjiwun: Flow ("it flows by")

Bizaanyan: Be Quiet

Bi-zhaun: Come

Dowaemah: Sister

Ehn: Yes

Gchi-tenhtenh: Bullfrog

Giizhik: Cedar

Giin: You

Gooskee: Wary ("he is wary")

Gooskewin: Wariness, Caution

Ka, Kaween: No

Kahminik: Wolf

Keenawind: We (all)

Kitchi : Big

Kitchi Manitou: God (great spirit)

Kookookoo: Owl

Kwezenhs: Girl

Makkii: Frog

Manda: This

Maukinauk: Snapping Turtle

Milwaukee: The Fine Earth

Misheekaen: Turtle

Mississippi: The Great Water

Mong: Loon

Mudjeekawis: Brother (elder)

Mukwoh: Bear

Mushkeeg: Swamp

Nanabush: The Protector (personage)

Neebin: Summer

Neen: I

Nibeesh: Water

Nibo: Die ("he dies")

Nikibeeshin: Submerge

Nimush: Dog

Ningik: Otter

Ningoshkauwin: Disappearance

N'Mishomiss: Grandfather (my)

N'Okomis: Grandmother (my)
N'Osse: Father (my)
Ogimauh: Leader (chief)
Ogimauquae: Leader, (female)
Okwanim: Dam
Onish'shin: Good
Pitchi: Robin
Tessanaugh: Girl
Tibi-geezis: Moon
Tugwaugih: Autumn
Umbae: Go (let's)
Wenesh Giin?: Who (are you)?
Waewae: Canada Goose
Wah-jusk: Muskrat
Waubezhaesh: Marten

Wauboose: Rabbit
Weesenidauh: Eat (let's)
Wiigwauss: Birch
Wingizwaush: Osprey
Wiyaunuk: Pond
Zaaghigan: Lake
Zaegiziwin: Fear
Zaudeek: Poplar
Zaugiwaewin: Love
Zeeginigae: Pour ("it pours out")
Zeegwung: Spring
Zhingwauk: Pine
Zogopoh: Snow ("it is snowing")